HalLoWeen HOwLs

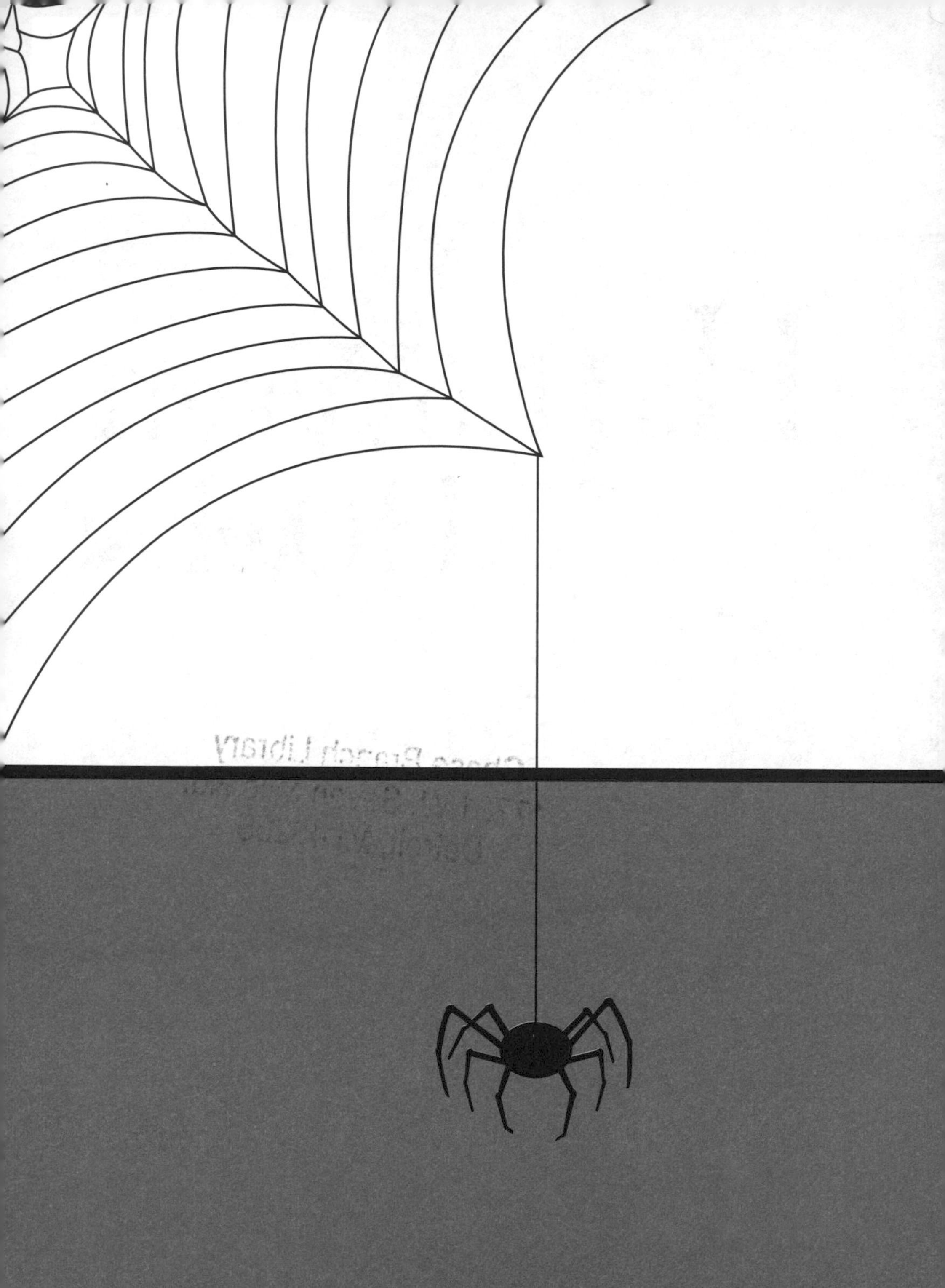

HalLoWeen HOwLs

Spooky Sounds, Stories & Songs

An Imprint of Sourcebooks, Inc.®
Naperville, Illinois

Edited, collected, and compiled by Megan Dempster, Mollie Denman, Laura Kuhn, and Alex Lubertozzi. "High Beams," "The Baby-Sitter," and "Cold As Clay" retold by Lubertozzi. "The Scarecrow" retold by Denman, Kuhn, and Lubertozzi.

Published by Sourcebooks, Inc.
P.O. Box 4410, Naperville, Illinois 60567-4410
(630) 961-3900
FAX: (630) 961-2168
www.sourcebooks.com

Library of Congress Cataloging-in-Publication Data
Halloween howls: spooky sounds, stories, and songs.
p. cm.
ISBN 1-4022-0193-1 (alk. paper)
1. Halloween. 2. Halloween—Songs and music. I. Sourcebooks, Inc.
GT4965 .H34 2003
810.8'0334—dc22
2003012719

Printed and bound in the United States of America
BG 10 9 8 7 6 5 4 3 2 1

Contents

CD Track List

Introduction

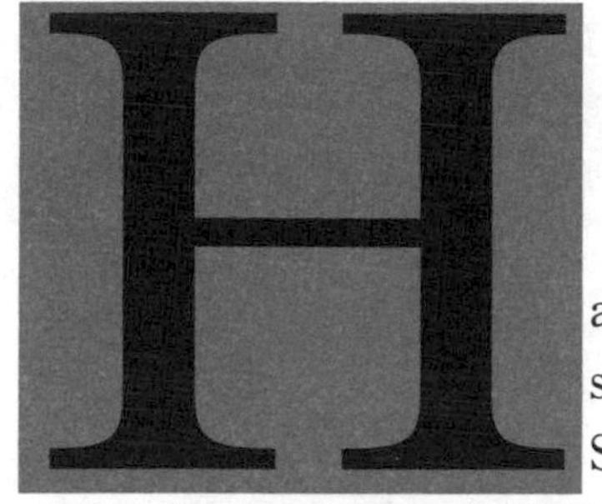

Halloween. What is it about this day that so fascinates young and old alike? Strange costumes, good food, scary stories....The origins of Halloween take us back to ancient Ireland and a Celtic fire festival known as "Samhain" (pronounced "sow-in"). Samhain, or All Hallowtide, was a feast of the dead that signaled the end of harvest and the onset of winter. On this night, the ghosts of the dead would trick humans into becoming lost in their burial mounds, where they would be trapped forever. Eventually, people began dressing up as these spirits, visiting people's houses and begging for treats. Those who refused would often become the victims of practical jokes. So Halloween has always had an element of playful wickedness, as well as a blurring of the boundary between the world of the living and of the dead.

When the Celts converted to Christianity, Pope Boniface IV designated November 1 as All Saints' Day, a day to honor the Christian saints and martyrs, as well as a way to replace the pagan festivals of the dead. The celebration was also called All Hallows. The night before—Samhain—became All Hallows' Eve, eventually "Halloween." When in A.D. 1000, the church made November 2 All Souls' Day, the three-day celebration of All

Hallows' Eve, All Saints' Day, and All Souls' Day became known as Hallowmas.

In America, however, it is All Hallows' Eve—Halloween—that has remained the center of our post-harvest celebrations. It is the one day of the year in which we can laugh at death and take pleasure in the morbid, the disturbing, the terrifying. Many Halloween traditions have become ingrained in our families and communities—getting together for good food and drink, trick-or-treating, dressing up in costumes, playing games, and telling scary stories.

This book is a collection of some of the best scary stories to tell and listen to on Halloween, as well as many fun things you can incorporate into your holiday festivities. The audio CD that comes with this book presents a handful of the stories told in chilling fashion, with spooky sounds and songs you can use on their own, or with your other favorite activities, on All Hallows' Eve. So put on your costume, turn out the lights, and be prepared to scare yourself silly!

The Editors

That story is creepy,
It's waily, it's weepy,
It's screechy and screamy
Right up to the end.
It's spooky, it's crawly,
It's grizzly, it's gory,
It's the *awfulest* story
(Please tell it again).

—*Shel Silverstein,*
"Blood-Curdling Story"

Halloween Howls

boom
boom
boom

I

The Tell-Tale Heart

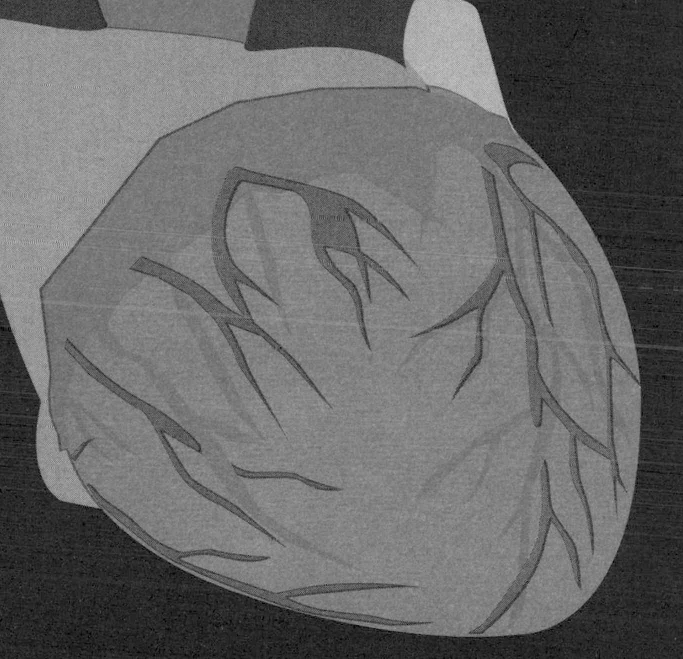

by Edgar Allan Poe

boom
boom

track 2

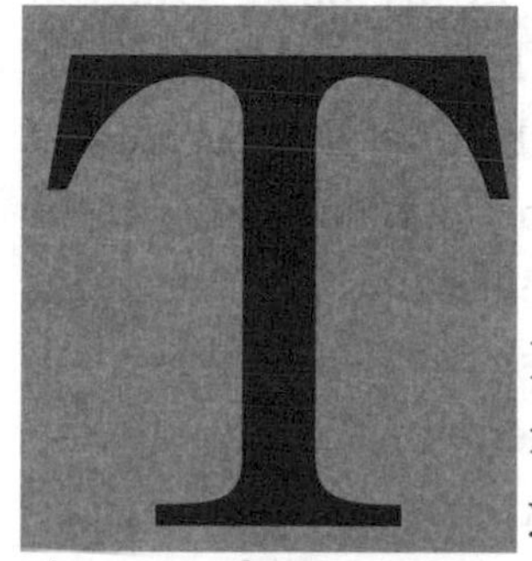

RUE!—nervous—very, very dreadfully nervous I had been and am; but why *will* you say that I am mad? The disease had sharpened my senses—not destroyed—not dulled them. Above all was the sense of hearing acute. I heard all things in the heaven and in the earth. I heard many things in hell. How, then, am I mad? Hearken! and observe how healthily—how calmly I can tell you the whole story.

It is impossible to say how first the idea entered my brain; but once conceived, it haunted me day and night. Object there was none. Passion there was none. I loved the old man. He had never wronged me. He had never given me insult. For his gold I had no desire. I think it was his eye! Yes, it was this! He had the eye of a vulture—a pale blue eye, with a film over it. Whenever it fell upon me, my blood ran cold; and so by degrees—very gradually—I made up my mind to take the life of the old man, and thus rid myself of the eye forever.

Now this is the point. You fancy me mad. Madmen know nothing. But you should have seen *me*. You should have seen how wisely I proceeded—with what caution—with what foresight—

with what dissimulation I went to work! I was never kinder to the old man than during the whole week before I killed him. And every night, about midnight, I turned the latch of his door and opened it—oh so gently! And then, when I had made an opening sufficient for my head, I put in a dark lantern, all closed, closed, that no light shone out, and then I thrust in my head. Oh, you would have laughed to see how cunningly I thrust it in! I moved it slowly—very, very slowly, so that I might not disturb the old man's sleep. It took me an hour to place my whole head within the opening so far that I could see him as he lay upon his bed. Ha! would a madman have been so wise as this? And then, when my head was well in the room, I undid the lantern cautiously—oh, so cautiously—cautiously (for the hinges creaked)—I undid it just so much that a single thin ray fell upon the vulture eye. And this I did for seven long nights—every night just at midnight—but I found the eye always closed; and so it was impossible to do the work; for it was not the old man who vexed me, but his Evil Eye. And every morning, when the day broke, I went boldly into the chamber, and spoke courageously to him, calling him by name in a hearty tone, and inquiring how he had passed the night. So you see he would have been a very profound old man, indeed, to suspect that every night, just at twelve, I looked in upon him while he slept.

Upon the eighth night I was more than usually cautious in opening the door. A watch's minute hand moves more quickly than did mine. Never before that night had I *felt* the extent of my own powers—of my sagacity. I could scarcely contain my feelings of triumph. To think that there I was, opening the door, little by little, and he not even to dream of my secret deeds or thoughts. I fairly chuckled at the idea; and perhaps he heard me; for he moved on the bed suddenly, as if startled. Now you may think that I drew back—but no. His room was as black as pitch with the thick darkness (for the shutters were close fastened, through fear of robbers), and so I knew that he could not see the opening of the door, and I kept pushing it on steadily, steadily.

I had my head in, and was about to open the lantern, when my thumb slipped upon the tin fastening, and the old man sprang up in the bed, crying out—"Who's there?"

I kept quite still and said nothing. For a whole hour I did not move a muscle, and in the meantime I did not hear him lie down. He was still sitting up in the bed listening;—just as I have done, night after night, hearkening to the death watches in the wall.

Presently I heard a slight groan, and I knew it was the groan of mortal terror. It was not a groan of pain or of grief—oh, no!—it was the low stifled sound that arises from the bottom of the soul when overcharged with awe. I knew the sound well. Many a night, just at midnight, when all the world slept, it has welled up from my own bosom, deepening, with its dreadful echo, the terrors that distracted me. I say I knew it well. I knew what the old man felt, and pitied him, although I chuckled at heart. I knew that he had been lying awake ever since the first slight noise, when he had turned in the bed. His fears had been ever since growing upon him. He had been trying to fancy them causeless, but could not. He had been saying to himself—"It is nothing but the wind in the chimney—it is only a mouse crossing the floor," or "it is merely a cricket which has made a single chirp." Yes, he has been trying to comfort himself with these suppositions: but he had found all in vain. *All in vain;* because Death, in approaching him, had stalked with his black shadow before him, and enveloped the victim. And it was the mournful influence of the unperceived shadow that caused him to feel—although he neither saw nor heard—to *feel* the presence of my head within the room.

When I had waited a long time, very patiently, without hearing him lie down, I resolved to open a little—a very, very little crevice in the lantern. So I opened it—you cannot imagine how stealthily, stealthily—until, at length, a simple dim ray, like the thread of the spider, shot from out the crevice and fell full upon the vulture eye.

It was open—wide, wide open—and I grew furious as I gazed upon it. I saw it with perfect distinctness—all a dull blue, with a hideous veil over it that chilled the very marrow in my bones; but I could see nothing else of the old man's face or person: for I had directed the ray as if by instinct, precisely upon the damned spot.

And now have I not told you that what you mistake for madness is but over-acuteness of the senses?—now, I say, there came to my ears a low, dull, quick sound, such as a watch makes when enveloped in cotton. I knew *that* sound well too. It was the beating of the old man's heart. It increased my fury, as the beating of a drum stimulates the soldier into courage.

But even yet I refrained and kept still. I scarcely breathed. I held the lantern motionless. I tried how steadily I could maintain the ray upon the eye. Meantime the hellish tattoo of the heart increased. It grew quicker and quicker, and louder and louder every instant. The old man's terror *must* have been extreme! It grew louder, I say, louder every moment!—do you mark me well? I have told you that I am nervous: so I am. And now at the dead hour of the night, amid the dreadful silence of that old house, so strange a noise as this excited me to uncontrollable terror. Yet, for some minutes longer I refrained and stood still. But the beating grew louder, louder! I thought the heart must burst. And now a new anxiety seized me—the sound would be heard by a neighbour! The old man's hour had come! With a loud yell, I threw open the lantern and leaped into the room. He shrieked once—once only. In an instant I dragged him to the floor, and pulled the heavy bed over him. I then smiled gaily, to find the deed so far done. But, for many minutes, the heart beat on with a muffled sound. This, however, did not vex me; it would not be heard through the wall. At length it ceased. The old man was dead. I removed the bed and examined the corpse. Yes, he was stone, stone dead. I placed my hand upon the heart and held it there many minutes. There was no pulsation. He was stone dead. His eye would trouble me no more.

If still you think me mad, you will think so no longer when I describe the wise precautions I took for the concealment of the body. The night waned, and I worked hastily, but in silence. First of all I dismembered the corpse. I cut off the head and the arms and the legs.

I then took up three planks from the flooring of the chamber, and deposited all between the scantlings. I then replaced the boards so cleverly, so cunningly, that no human eye—not even *his*—could have detected any thing wrong. There was nothing to wash out—no stain of any kind—no blood-spot whatever. I had been too wary for that. A tub had caught all—ha! ha!

When I had made an end of these labors, it was four o'clock—still dark as midnight. As the bell sounded the hour, there came a knocking at the street door. I went down to open it with a light heart,—for what had I *now* to fear? There entered three men, who introduced themselves, with perfect suavity, as officers of the police. A shriek had been heard by a neighbour during the night; suspicion of foul play had been aroused; information had been lodged at the police office, and they (the officers) had been deputed to search the premises.

I smiled,—for *what* had I to fear? I bade the gentlemen welcome. The shriek, I said, was my own in a dream. The old man, I mentioned, was absent in the country. I took my visitors all over the house. I bade them search—search *well.* I led them, at length, to *his* chamber. I showed them his treasures, secure, undisturbed. In the enthusiasm of my confidence, I brought chairs into the room, and desired them *here* to rest from their fatigues, while I myself, in the wild audacity of my perfect triumph, placed my own seat upon the very spot beneath which reposed the corpse of the victim.

The officers were satisfied. My *manner* had convinced them. I was singularly at ease. They sat, and while I answered cheerily, they chatted of familiar things. But, ere long, I felt myself getting pale and wished them gone. My head ached, and I fancied a ringing in my ears: but still they sat and still chatted. The ringing became more distinct:—it continued and became more distinct: I talked more freely to get rid of the feeling: but it continued and gained definitiveness—until, at length, I found that the noise was *not* within my ears.

No doubt I now grew *very* pale;—but I talked more fluently, and with a heightened voice. Yet the sound increased—and what could I do? It was *a low, dull, quick sound—much such a sound as a watch makes when enveloped in cotton.* I gasped for breath—and yet the officers heard it not. I talked more quickly—more vehemently; but the noise steadily increased. I arose and argued about trifles, in a high key and with violent gesticulations; but the noise steadily increased. Why *would* they not be gone? I paced the floor to and fro with heavy strides, as if excited to fury by the observations of the men—but the noise steadily increased. Oh God! what *could* I do? I foamed—I raved—I swore! I swung the chair upon which I had been sitting, and grated it upon the boards, but the noise arose over all and continually increased. It grew louder—louder—*louder!* And still the men chatted pleasantly, and smiled. Was it possible they heard not? Almighty God!—no, no! They heard!—they suspected!—they *knew!*—they were making a mockery of my horror!—this I thought, and this I think. But anything was better than this agony! Anything was more tolerable than this derision! I could bear those hypocritical smiles no longer! I felt that I must scream or die!—and now—again!—hark! louder! louder! louder! *louder!*—

"Villains!" I shrieked, "dissemble no more! I admit the deed!—tear up the planks! here, here!—it is the beating of his hideous heart!"

Scary Halloween Costumes

Mummy

1. Start with a white pair of pants and white T-shirt

2. Tear long, thin (2"–3" wide) strips from a white bed sheet and have someone help wrap your legs, arms, and torso with the strips. Tie the ends or use safety pins to keep them in place.

3. For an extra moldy appearance, you can age the sheet by dyeing it a very light gray (or just drag it around in the dirt for a while) and fray the edges of the strips. Make sure to wrap your feet, hands, and fingers, leaving some of the strips loose to give a slightly unraveled look.

4. You should wrap your head, but be careful not to cover your eyes, ears, nose, or mouth. Paint your face white, with dark circles around your eyes, and sprinkle your hair and wrappings with baby powder to complete the "undead" effect.

Spider

1. Start with a black sweatsuit

2. Get two pairs of black tights or thick nylons. Cut the legs off the tights and stuff each leg with Fiberfil until each is as long as the sleeves of the sweatshirt.

3. Position two filled legs on each side of the sweatshirt, evenly spaced below the arms. You can attach them with safety pins or sew them onto the sweatshirt.

4. Once the extra "legs" are attached, use thick black thread or fishing line to tie the end and middle of each leg to each other. Leave enough slack so that the legs hang freely of one another.

5. Attach each top leg to the wrist and elbow of the person wearing the costume, again leaving enough slack. Now the person will have eight "legs" just like a spider, with the ones on top moving in concert with the person's arms.

6. Paint the face black, or put on a black ski mask. For a nice, added touch, wear black gloves and fangs.

The Monkey's Paw

2

by W.W. Jacobs

creeeak

Without, the night was cold and wet, but in the small parlour of Laburnam Villa the blinds were drawn and the fire burned brightly. Father and son were at chess, the former, who possessed ideas about the game involving radical changes, putting his king into such sharp and unnecessary perils that it even provoked comment from the white-haired old lady knitting placidly by the fire.

"Hark at the wind," said Mr. White, who, having seen a fatal mistake after it was too late, was amiably desirous of preventing his son from seeing it.

"I'm listening," said the latter, grimly surveying the board as he stretched out his hand. "Check."

"I should hardly think that he'd come to-night," said his father, with his hand poised over the board.

"Mate," replied the son.

"That's the worst of living so far out," bawled Mr. White, with sudden and unlooked-for violence; "of all the beastly, slushy, out-of-the-way places to live in, this is the worst. Pathway's a bog, and the road's a torrent. I don't know what people are thinking about. I suppose because only two houses on the road are let, they think it doesn't matter."

"Never mind, dear," said his wife soothingly; "perhaps you'll win the next one."

Mr. White looked up sharply, just in time to intercept a knowing glance between mother and son. The words died away on his lips, and he hid a guilty grin in his thin grey beard.

"There he is," said Herbert White, as the gate banged too loudly, and heavy footsteps came toward the door.

The old man rose with hospitable haste, and opening the door, was heard condoling with the new arrival. The new arrival also condoled with himself, so that Mrs. White said, "Tut, tut!" and coughed gently as her husband entered the room, followed by a tall burly man, beady of eye and rubicund of visage.

"Sergeant-Major Morris," he said, introducing him.

The sergeant-major shook hands, and taking the proffered seat by the fire, watched contentedly while his host got out whisky and tumblers and stood a small copper kettle on the fire.

At the third glass his eyes got brighter, and he began to talk, the little family circle regarding with eager interest this visitor from distant parts, as he squared his broad shoulders in the chair and spoke of strange scenes and doughty deeds; of wars and plagues and strange peoples.

"Twenty-one years of it," said Mr. White, nodding at his wife and son. "When he went away he was a slip of a youth in the warehouse. Now look at him."

"He don't look to have taken much harm," said Mrs. White, politely.

"I'd like to go to India myself," said the old man, "just to look round a bit, you know."

"Better where you are," said the sergeant-major, shaking his head. He put down the empty glass, and sighing softly, shook it again.

"I should like to see those old temples and fakirs and jugglers," said the old man. "What was that you started telling me the other day about a monkey's paw or something, Morris?"

"Nothing," said the soldier hastily. "Leastways, nothing worth hearing."

"Monkey's paw?" said Mrs. White curiously.

"Well, it's just a bit of what you might call magic, perhaps," said the sergeant-major, off-handedly.

His three listeners leaned forward eagerly. The visitor absent-mindedly put his empty glass to his lips and then set it down again. His host filled it for him.

"To look at," said the sergeant-major, fumbling in his pocket, "it's just an ordinary little paw, dried to a mummy."

He took something out of his pocket and proffered it. Mrs. White drew back with a grimace, but her son, taking it, examined it curiously.

"And what is there special about it?" inquired Mr. White, as he took it from his son and, having examined it, placed it upon the table.

"It had a spell put on it by an old fakir," said the sergeant-major, "a very holy man. He wanted to show that fate ruled people's lives, and that those who interfered with it did so to their sorrow. He put a spell on it so that three separate men could each have three wishes from it."

His manner was so impressive that his hearers were conscious that their light laughter jarred somewhat.

"Well, why don't you have three, sir?" said Herbert White cleverly.

The soldier regarded him in the way that middle age is wont to regard presumptuous youth. "I have," he said quietly, and his blotchy face whitened.

"And did you really have the three wishes granted?" asked Mrs. White.

"I did," said the sergeant-major, and his glass tapped against his strong teeth.

"And has anybody else wished?" inquired the old lady.

"The first man had his three wishes, yes," was the reply. "I don't know what the first two were, but the third was for death. That's how I got the paw."

His tones were so grave that a hush fell upon the group.

"If you've had your three wishes, it's no good to you now, then, Morris," said the old man at last. "What do you keep it for?"

The soldier shook his head. "Fancy, I suppose," he said slowly.

"If you could have another three wishes," said the old man, eyeing him keenly, "would you have them?"

"I don't know," said the other. "I don't know."

He took the paw, and dangling it between his front finger and thumb, suddenly threw it upon the fire. White, with a slight cry, stooped down and snatched it off.

"Better let it burn," said the soldier solemnly.

"If you don't want it, Morris," said the old man, "give it to me."

"I won't," said his friend doggedly. "I threw it on the fire. If you keep it, don't blame me for what happens. Pitch it on the fire again, like a sensible man."

The other shook his head and examined his new possession closely. "How do you do it?" he inquired.

"Hold it up in your right hand and wish aloud," said the sergeant-major, "but I warn you of the consequences."

"Sounds like the *Arabian Nights*," said Mrs. White, as she rose and began to set the supper. "Don't you think you might wish for four pairs of hands for me?"

Her husband drew the talisman from his pocket, and then all three burst into laughter as the sergeant-major, with a look of alarm on his face, caught him by the arm.

"If you must wish," he said gruffly, "wish for something sensible."

Mr. White dropped it back into his pocket, and placing chairs, motioned his friend to the table. In the business of supper the talisman was partly forgotten, and afterward the three sat listening in an enthralled fashion to a second installment of the soldier's adventures in India.

"If the tale about the monkey paw is not more truthful than those he has been telling us," said Herbert, as the door closed behind their guest, just in time for him to catch the last train, "we shan't make much out of it."

"Did you give him anything for it, Father?" inquired Mrs. White, regarding her husband closely.

"A trifle," said he, colouring slightly. "He didn't want it, but I made him take it. And he pressed me again to throw it away."

"Likely," said Herbert, with pretended horror. "Why, we're going to be rich, and famous, and happy. Wish to be an emperor, father, to begin with; then you can't be henpecked."

He darted round the table, pursued by the maligned Mrs. White armed with an antimacassar.

Mr. White took the paw from his pocket and eyed it dubiously. "I don't know what to wish for, and that's a fact," he said slowly. "It seems to me I've got all I want."

"If you only cleared the house, you'd be quite happy, wouldn't you?" said Herbert, with his hand on his shoulder. "Well, wish for two hundred pounds, then; that'll just do it."

His father, smiling shamefacedly at his own credulity, held up the talisman, as his son, with a solemn face somewhat marred by a wink at his mother, sat down at the piano and struck a few impressive chords.

"I wish for two hundred pounds," said the old man distinctly.

A fine crash from the piano greeted the words, interrupted by a shuddering cry from the old man. His wife and son ran toward him.

"It moved, he cried, with a glance of disgust at the object as it lay on the floor. "As I wished, it twisted in my hands like a snake."

"Well, I don't see the money," said his son, as he picked it up and placed it on the table, "and I bet I never shall."

"It must have been your fancy, Father," said his wife, regarding him anxiously.

He shook his head. "Never mind, though; there's no harm done, but it gave me a shock all the same."

They sat down by the fire again while the two men finished their pipes. Outside, the wind was higher than ever, and the old man started nervously at the sound of a door banging upstairs. A silence unusual and depressing settled upon all three, which lasted until the old couple rose to retire for the night.

"I expect you'll find the cash tied up in a big bag in the middle of your bed," said Herbert, as he bade them good-night, "and something horrible squatting up on top of the wardrobe watching you as you pocket your ill-gotten gains."

He sat alone in the darkness, gazing at the dying fire, and seeing faces in it. The last face was so horrible and so simian that he gazed at it in amazement. It got so vivid that, with a little uneasy laugh, he felt on the table for a glass containing a little water to throw over it. His hand grasped the monkey's paw, and with a little shiver he wiped his hand on his coat and went up to bed.

II.

In the brightness of the wintry sun the next morning as it streamed over the breakfast table, Herbert laughed at his fears. There was an air of prosaic wholesomeness about the room which it had lacked on the previous night, and the dirty, shrivelled little paw was pitched on the sideboard with a carelessness which betokened no great belief in its virtues.

"I suppose all old soldiers are the same," said Mrs White. "The idea of our listening to such nonsense! How could wishes be granted in these days? And if they could, how could two hundred pounds hurt you, Father?"

"Might drop on his head from the sky," said the frivolous Herbert.

"Morris said the things happened so naturally," said his father, "that you might if you so wished attribute it to coincidence."

"Well, don't break into the money before I come back," said Herbert, as he rose from the table. "I'm afraid it'll turn you into a mean, avaricious man, and we shall have to disown you."

His mother laughed, and following him to the door, watched him down the road, and returning to the breakfast table, was very happy at the expense of her husband's credulity. All of which did not prevent her from scurrying to the door at the postman's knock, nor prevent her from referring somewhat shortly to retired sergeant-majors of bibulous habits when she found that the post brought a tailor's bill.

"Herbert will have some more of his funny remarks, I expect, when he comes home," she said, as they sat at dinner.

"I dare say," said Mr. White, pouring himself out some beer; "but for all that, the thing moved in my hand; that I'll swear to."

"You thought it did," said the old lady soothingly.

"I say it did," replied the other. "There was no thought about it; I had just—What's the matter?"

His wife made no reply. She was watching the mysterious movements of a man outside, who, peering in an undecided fashion at the house, appeared to be trying to make up his mind to enter. In mental connection with the two hundred pounds, she noticed that the stranger was well dressed and wore a silk hat of glossy newness. Three times he paused at the gate, and then walked on again. The fourth time he stood with his hand upon it and then with sudden resolution flung it open and walked up the path. Mrs. White at the same moment placed her hands behind her and, hurriedly unfastening the strings of her apron, put that useful article of apparel beneath the cushion of her chair.

She brought the stranger, who seemed ill at ease, into the room. He gazed at her furtively and listened in a preoccupied fashion as the old lady apologized for the appearance of the room, and her husband's coat, a garment which he usually reserved for the garden. She then waited as patiently as her sex would permit for him to broach his business, but he was at first strangely silent.

"I—was asked to call," he said at last, and stooped and picked a piece of cotton from his trousers. "I come from Maw and Meggins."

The old lady started. "Is anything the matter?" she asked, breathlessly. "Has anything happened to Herbert? What is it? What is it?"

Her husband interposed. "There, there, mother," he said hastily. "Sit down, and don't jump to conclusions. You've not brought bad news, I'm sure, sir," and he eyed the other wistfully.

"I'm sorry—" began the visitor.

"Is he hurt?" demanded the mother.

The visitor bowed in assent. "Badly hurt," he said quietly, "but he is not in any pain."

"Oh, thank God!" said the old woman, clasping her hands. "Thank God for that! Thank—"

She broke off suddenly as the sinister meaning of the assurance dawned upon her and she saw the awful confirmation of her fears in the other's averted face. She caught her breath, and turning to her slower-witted husband, laid her trembling old hand upon his. There was a long silence.

"He was caught in the machinery," said the visitor at length, in a low voice.

"Caught in the machinery," repeated Mr. White, in a dazed fashion, "yes."

He sat staring blankly out the window, and taking his wife's hand between his own, pressed it as he had been wont to do in their old courting days nearly forty years before.

"He was the only one left to us," he said, turning gently to the visitor. "It is hard."

The other coughed, and rising, walked slowly to the window. "The firm wished me to convey their sincere sympathy with you in your great loss," he said, without looking round. "I beg that you will understand I am only their servant and merely obeying orders."

There was no reply; the old woman's face was white, her eyes staring, and her breath inaudible; on the husband's face was a look such as his friend the sergeant might have carried into his first action.

"I was to say that Maw and Meggins disclaim all responsibility," continued the other. "They admit no liability at all, but in consideration of your son's services, they wish to present you with a certain sum as compensation."

Mr. White dropped his wife's hand, and rising to his feet, gazed with a look of horror at his visitor. His dry lips shaped the words, "How much?"

"Two hundred pounds," was the answer.

Unconscious of his wife's shriek, the old man smiled faintly, put out his hands like a sightless man, and dropped, a senseless heap, to the floor.

III.

In the huge new cemetery, some two miles distant, the old people buried their dead and came back to a house steeped in shadow and silence. It was all over so quickly that at first they could hardly realize it and remained in a state of expectation as though of something else to happen—something else which was to lighten this load, too heavy for old hearts to bear.

But the days passed, and expectation gave place to resignation—the hopeless resignation of the old, sometimes miscalled apathy. Sometimes they hardly exchanged a word, for now they had nothing to talk about, and their days were long to weariness.

It was about a week after that that the old man, waking suddenly in the night, stretched out his hand and found himself alone. The room was in darkness, and the sound of subdued weeping came from the window. He raised himself in bed and listened.

"Come back," he said tenderly. "You will be cold."

"It is colder for my son," said the old woman, and wept afresh.

The sound of her sobs died away on his ears. The bed was warm and his eyes heavy with sleep. He dozed fitfully and then slept until a sudden wild cry from his wife awoke him with a start.

"*The paw!*" she cried wildly. "The monkey's paw!"

He started up in alarm. "Where? Where is it? What's the matter?"

She came stumbling across the room toward him. "I want it," she said quietly. "You've not destroyed it?"

"It's in the parlour, on the bracket," he replied, marvelling. "Why?"

She cried and laughed together, and bending over, kissed his cheek.

"I only just thought of it," she said hysterically. "Why didn't I think of it before? Why didn't *you* think of it?"

"Think of what?" he questioned.

"The other two wishes," she replied rapidly. "We've only had one."

"Was not that enough?" he demanded fiercely.

"No," she cried, triumphantly; "we'll have one more. Go down and get it quickly, and wish our boy alive again."

The man sat up in bed and flung the bedclothes from his quaking limbs. "Good God, you are mad!" he cried aghast.

"Get it," she panted; "get it quickly, and wish—Oh, my boy, my boy!"

Her husband struck a match and lit the candle. "Get back to bed," he said, unsteadily. "You don't know what you are saying."

"We had the first wish granted," said the old woman, feverishly; "why not the second?"

"A coincidence," stammered the old man.

"Go and get it and wish," cried the old woman, quivering with excitement.

The old man turned and regarded her, and his voice shook. "He has been dead ten days, and besides he—I would not tell you else, but—I could only recognize him by his clothing. If he was too terrible for you to see then, how now?"

"Bring him back," cried the old woman, and dragged him toward the door. "Do you think I fear the child I have nursed?"

He went down in the darkness and felt his way to the parlour and then to the mantelpiece. The talisman was in its place, and a horrible fear that the unspoken wish might bring his mutilated son before him ere he could escape from the room seized upon him, and he caught his breath as he found that he had lost the direction of the door. His brow cold with sweat, he felt his way round the table and groped along the wall until he found himself in the small passage with the unwholesome thing in his hand.

Even his wife's face seemed changed as he entered the room. It was white and expectant, and to his fears seemed to have an unnatural look upon it. He was afraid of her.

"*Wish!*" she cried, in a strong voice.

"It is foolish and wicked," he faltered.

"*Wish!*" repeated his wife.

He raised his hand. "I wish my son alive again."

The talisman fell to the floor, and he regarded it fearfully. Then he sank trembling into a chair as the old woman, with burning eyes, walked to the window and raised the blind.

He sat until he was chilled with the cold, glancing occasionally at the figure of the old woman peering through the window. The candle end, which had burnt below the rim of the china candlestick, was throwing pulsating shadows on the ceiling and walls, until, with a flicker larger than the rest, it expired. The old man, with an unspeakable sense of relief at the failure of the talisman, crept back to his bed, and a minute or two afterward the old woman came silently and apathetically beside him.

Neither spoke, but both lay silently listening to the ticking of the clock. A stair creaked, and a squeaky mouse scurried noisily through the wall. The darkness was oppressive, and after lying for some time screwing up his courage, the husband took the box of matches, and striking one, went downstairs for a candle.

At the foot of the stairs the match went out, and he paused to strike another, and at the same moment a knock, so quiet and stealthy as to be scarcely audible, sounded on the front door.

The matches fell from his hand. He stood motionless, his breath suspended until the knock was repeated. Then he turned and fled swiftly back to his room, and closed the door behind him. A third knock sounded through the house.

"*What's that?*" cried the old woman, starting up.

"A rat," said the old man, in shaking tones—"a rat. It passed me on the stairs."

His wife sat up in bed listening. A loud knock resounded through the house.

"It's Herbert!" she screamed. "It's Herbert!"

She ran to the door, but her husband was before her, and catching her by the arm, held her tightly.

"What are you going to do?" he whispered hoarsely.

"It's my boy; it's Herbert!" she cried, struggling mechanically. "I forgot it was two miles away. What are you holding me for? Let go. I must open the door."

"For God's sake, don't let it in," cried the old man, trembling.

"You're afraid of your own son," she cried, struggling. "Let me go. I'm coming, Herbert; I'm coming."

There was another knock, and another. The old woman with a sudden wrench broke free and ran from the room. Her husband followed to the landing and called after her appealingly as she hurried downstairs. He heard the chain rattle back and the bottom bolt drawn slowly and stiffly from the socket. Then the old woman's voice, strained and panting.

"The bolt," she cried loudly. "Come down. I can't reach it."

But her husband was on his hands and knees groping wildly on the floor in search of the paw. If he could only find it before the thing outside got in. A perfect fusillade of knocks reverberated through the house, and he heard the scraping of a chair as his wife put it down in the passage against the door. He heard the creaking of the bolt as it came slowly back, and at the same moment he found the monkey's paw and frantically breathed his third and last wish.

The knocking ceased suddenly, although the echoes of it were still in the house. He heard the chair drawn back and the door opened. A cold wind rushed up the staircase, and a long loud wail of disappointment and misery from his wife gave him courage to run down to her side and then to the gate beyond. The street lamp flickering opposite shone on a quiet and deserted road.

Just Plain Silly Halloween Costumes

Magic 8 Ball

1. Dress all in black (a black turtleneck works well), including black gloves to cover your hands.

2. Cut out white construction-paper triangles, and write fun fortunes, such as, "Most Definitely," "Outlook Not So Good," "Better Not Tell You Now," "Don't Count on It," and "Check Back Later." Be creative!

3. Tape these triangles to your clothes.

4. Draw a number *8* on your forehead or cheek with makeup.

Bunch of Grapes

1. Dress all in purple or green (depending on which type of grapes you want to be).

2. Find coordinating latex balloons (blown up with air, not helium—unless you want to float away!).

3. Attach the ends of the balloons to your clothing with safety pins. They should bunched up fairly close together, but not so thick that you can't move around.

4. Top the look off with a matching purple or green hat, and watch out for tree branches while trick-or-treating!

3

High Beams

a folk tale

Laura, an eighteen-year-old freshman attending college in Iowa, was returning to her home in Illinois for Thanksgiving. Because her last class had ended late in the afternoon, she had to make the five-hour trip at night. Driving alone in the old green sedan her parents had given her when she had left home for school, she was worried about staying awake on the endless expanse of interstate that lay between school and her parents' house. Halfway home, she decided to get off the freeway to stretch her legs and gas up the car.

It was a run-down little filling station in the middle of nowhere. She got out of her car and shivered at the brisk November air. While she filled her tank, she noticed a red pickup truck pull up to one of the pumps. The pickup was older than her own car and had a large dent on the front bumper. The man who got out of the truck was wearing a cap that almost covered his eyes, and she could see that his face was deeply lined and pocked, and that he hadn't shaved in several days.

When she finished pumping, she went inside to pay. The man behind the counter seemed a kindly old sort, and she asked him if there was a good alternative to the four-lane freeway that was putting her to sleep.

"Route 71 runs parallel to the interstate for about a hundred miles. You can get back on near Rockford, and you'll almost be home."

She thanked the man, got back into her car, and started down the winding, two-lane highway. For a while, she was the only car on the road. Then she noticed a pair of headlights off in the distance in her rearview mirror. The lights would disappear behind a hill and then reappear. Gradually, the lights grew closer and closer, until they were no more than ten feet behind her. She slowed down to let the other driver pass. But he did not pass.

Then she noticed that the car behind her was the red pickup she'd seen at the filling station. It had the same dent in the fender, and the driver was wearing a baseball cap pulled down to his eyes. She tensed up and pressed her foot on the accelerator, but the truck sped up with her, staying close to her bumper. Suddenly, he turned on his high beams, flooding her car with light. She began to get nervous and started driving faster, hoping to lose the truck, but he stayed with her, flashing his beams on and off at her.

"What does he want from me?" she said to herself, becoming truly frightened for the first time. She tried slowing down again, but he would not pass or back off. He continued to flash his headlights at odd intervals.

Finally, he began to pass her on the left, but once he was beside her, he stayed there. *What is he doing?* she thought. He was motioning toward her, pointing at her and then at the shoulder. He wanted her to pull over, but she was deathly afraid of the man and felt certain that if she stopped, he would kill her.

She sped up again, and he fell behind her as the road curved. She could see that they were headed to a quiet little town that straddled the highway. She decided she would try to lose him down a side street once they reached an intersection. She took a hard right at thirty miles an hour down the first street she came upon. She could see the truck fly past her, surprised by her turn. The truck's wheels locked and skidded on the shoulder as its nose dipped down and brake lights glowed red. In a panic, she floored the gas and raced down the tree-lined street of Victorian houses with wide front porches and frosted lawns. She knew that the truck was still chasing her, so she quickly turned left and then took two right turns to head back to the highway. In her rearview mirror, she was sure she saw him speeding down the road she had just turned off, heading away from her. She could see the sign for Route 71 and careened the old green sedan toward the highway and back to the interstate. Her heart racing, she decided she'd had enough of the local roads.

Behind the wheel of his red pickup truck, the driver cursed and continued searching for the girl in the green sedan. He was desperate to find her and despondent that he couldn't get her to pull over.

Earlier, as he was walking back to his pickup after paying the attendant at the gas station, he noticed her pulling out onto the road. And he swore he saw the figure of a man crouched in the backseat, holding something shiny, metallic. He rushed into his truck and hurried to catch up with her. When he got close, he could see that there was indeed a man hiding in her backseat. The man raised up to the girl, holding a long straight razor in his right hand. That's when the driver turned on his high beams. Each time he did, the man sank back down into his seat. He tried to get her to pull over, but she must have been too afraid.

The driver reported her car and license plate to the local police, but the car and the girl were never found. The madman in the backseat had slit her throat on Route 71 and sunk the green sedan in a pond. The last thought that ran through Laura's mind was the realization that the man in the pickup truck wasn't trying to hurt her, he was trying to save her.

The Hearse Song

Don't you ever laugh as the hearse goes by,
For you may be the next to die.
They wrap you up in a big white sheet
From your head down to your naked feet.
They put you in a big black box
And cover you up with dirt and rocks.
All goes well for about a week,
But then your coffin begins to leak.
The worms crawl in, the worms crawl out,
The worms play pinochle on your snout.
They eat your eyes, they eat your toes,
They eat the jelly inside your nose.
An ugly green worm of unusual size
Crawls in your stomach and out your eyes.
Your stomach turns a slimy green,
And pus pours out like whipping cream.
You spread it on a slice of bread,
And that's what you eat when you are dead.

4

The Judge's House

by Bram Stoker

eeeeeeek

hen the time for his examination drew near, Malcolm Malcolmson made up his mind to go somewhere to read by himself. He feared the attractions of the seaside, and also he feared completely rural isolation, for of old he knew its harms, and so he determined to find some unpretentious little town where there would be nothing to distract him. He refrained from asking suggestions from any of his friends, for he argued that each would recommend some place of which he had knowledge and where he already had acquaintances. As Malcolmson wished to avoid friends, he had no wish to encumber himself with the attention of friends' friends, and so he determined to look out for a place for himself. He packed a large suitcase with some clothes and all the books he required, and then took a ticket for the first name on the local timetable which he did not know.

When at the end of three hours' journey he alighted at Benchurch, he felt satisfied that he had so far obliterated his tracks as to be sure of having a peaceful opportunity of pursuing his studies. He went straight to the one inn which the sleepy little place contained, and put up for the night. Benchurch was a market town, and once in three weeks was crowded to excess, but for the remainder of the twenty-one days it was as attractive as a desert. Malcolmson looked around the day after his arrival to try to find quarters more isolated than even so quiet an inn as "The Good Traveller" afforded. There was only one place which took his fancy, and it certainly satisfied his wildest ideas regarding quiet; in fact, quiet was not the proper word to apply to it—desolation was the only term conveying any suitable idea of its isolation. It was an old, rambling, heavy-built house of the Jacobean style, with heavy gables and windows, unusually small, and set higher than was customary in such houses, and was surrounded with a high brick wall massively built. Indeed, on examination, it looked more like a fortified house than an ordinary dwelling. But all these things pleased Malcolmson. "Here," he thought, "is the very spot I have been looking for, and if I can get opportunity of using it I shall be happy." His joy was increased when he realised beyond doubt that it was not at present inhabited.

From the post office he got the name of the agent, who was rarely surprised at the application to rent a part of the old house. Mr. Carnford, the local lawyer and agent, was a genial old gentleman, and frankly confessed his delight at anyone being willing to live in the house.

"To tell you the truth," said he, "I should be only too happy, on behalf of the owners, to let anyone have the house rent free for a term of years if only to accustom the people here to see it inhabited. It has been so long empty that some kind of absurd prejudice has grown up about it, and this can be best put down by its occupation—if only," he added with a sly glance at Malcolmson, "by a scholar like yourself, who wants its quiet for a time."

Malcolmson thought it needless to ask the agent about the "absurd prejudice"; he knew he would get more information, if he should require it, on that subject from other quarters. He paid his three months' rent, got a receipt and the name of an old woman who would probably undertake to "do" for him, and came away with the keys in his pocket. He then went to the landlady of the inn, who was a cheerful and most kindly person, and asked her advice as to such stores and provisions as he would be likely to require. She threw up her hands in amazement when he told her where he was going to settle himself.

"Not in the Judge's House!" she said, and grew pale as she spoke. He explained the locality of the house, saying that he did not know its name. When he had finished she answered:

"Aye, sure enough—sure enough the very place! It is the Judge's House, sure enough." He asked her to tell him about the place, why so called, and what there was against it. She told him that it was so called locally because it had been many years before—how long she could not say, as she was herself from another part of the country, but she thought it must have been a hundred years or more—the abode of a judge who was held in great terror on account of his harsh sentences and his hostility to prisoners at Assizes. As to what there was against the house itself, she could not tell.

"It is too bad of me, sir, and you—and a young gentleman, too—if you will pardon me saying it, going to live there all alone. If you were my boy—and you'll excuse me for saying it—you wouldn't sleep there a night, not if I had to go there myself and pull the big alarm bell that's on that roof!"

After his examination of the house, Malcolmson decided to take up his abode in the great dining-room, which was big enough to serve for all his requirements; and Mrs. Witham, the landlady, with the aid of the charwoman, Mrs. Dempster, proceeded to arrange matters. Before going, she expressed all sorts of kind wishes, and at the door turned and said:

"And perhaps, sir, as the room is big and drafty it might be well to have one of those big screens put round your bed at night—though, truth to tell, I would die myself if I were to be so shut in with all kinds of—of 'things,' that put their heads round the sides, or over the top, and look on me!" The image which she had called up was too much for her nerves, and she fled incontinently.

Mrs. Dempster sniffed in a superior manner as the landlady disappeared, and remarked that for her own part she wasn't afraid of all the bogies in the kingdom.

"I'll tell you what it is, sir," she said; "bogies is all kinds and sorts of things—except bogies! Rats and mice, and beetles, and creaky doors, and loose slates, and broken panes, and stiff drawer handles that stay out when you pull them and then fall down in the middle of the night. Look at the wainscot of the room! It is old—hundreds of years old! Do you think there's no rats and beetles there! And do you imagine, sir, that you won't see none of them? Rats is bogies, I tell you, and bogies is rats; and don't you get to think anything else!"

"My good woman," said Malcolmson hastily, "I have come here on purpose to obtain solitude; and believe me that I am grateful to the late Greenhow for having so organised his admirable charity—whatever it is—that I am perforce denied the opportunity of suffering from such a form of temptation! Saint Anthony himself could not be more rigid on the point!"

The old woman laughed harshly. "Ah, you young gentlemen," she said, "you don't fear for naught; and you'll get all the solitude you want here." She set to work with her cleaning; and by nightfall, when Malcolmson returned from his walk—he always had one of his books to study as he walked—he found the room swept and tidied, a fire burning in the old hearth, the lamp lit, and the table spread for supper with Mrs. Witham's excellent fare. "This is comfort, indeed," he said, as he rubbed his hands.

When he had finished his supper and lifted the tray to the other end of the great oak dining-table, he got out his books again, put fresh wood on the fire, trimmed his lamp, and set himself down to a spell of real hard work. He went on without pause till about eleven o'clock, when he knocked off for a bit to fix his fire and lamp, and to make himself a cup of tea. The renewed fire leaped and sparkled, and threw quaint shadows through the great old room; and as he sipped his hot tea, he revelled in the sense of isolation from his kind. Then it was that he began to notice for the first time what a noise the rats were making.

"Surely," he thought, "they cannot have been at it all the time I was reading. Had they been, I must have noticed it!" Presently, when the noise increased, he satisfied himself that it was really new. It was evident that at first the rats had been frightened at the presence of a stranger and the light of fire and lamp; but that as the time went on they had grown bolder and were now disporting themselves as was their wont.

How busy they were! And hark to the strange noises! Up and down behind the old wainscot, over the ceiling and under the floor they raced, and gnawed, and scratched! Malcolmson smiled to himself as he recalled to mind the saying of Mrs. Dempster, "Bogies is rats, and rats is bogies!" The tea began to have its effect of intellectual and nervous stimulus; he saw with joy another long spell of work to be done before the night was past, and in the sense of security which it gave him, he allowed himself the luxury of a good look round the room. He took his lamp in one hand and went all around, wondering that so quaint and beautiful an old house had been so long neglected. The carving of the oak on the panels of the wainscot was fine, and on and round the doors and windows it was beautiful and of rare merit. There were some old pictures on the walls, but they were coated so thick with dust and dirt that he could not distinguish any detail of them, though he held his lamp as high as he could over his head. Here and there as he went round he saw some crack or hole blocked for a moment by the face of a rat with its bright eyes glittering in the light, but in an instant it was gone, and a squeak and a scamper followed. The thing that most struck him, however, was the rope of the great alarm bell on the roof, which hung down in a corner of the room on the right-hand side of the fireplace. He pulled up close to the hearth a great high-backed carved oak chair and sat down to his last cup of tea. When this was done, he made up the fire and went back to his work, sitting at the corner of the table, having the fire to his left. For a little while the rats disturbed him somewhat with their perpetual scampering, but he got accustomed to the noise as one does to the ticking of a clock or to the roar of moving water, and he became so immersed in his work that everything in the world, except the problem which he was trying to solve, passed away from him.

He suddenly looked up; his problem was still unsolved, and there was in the air that sense of the hour before the dawn, which is so dread to doubtful life. The noise of the rats had ceased. Indeed it seemed to him that it must have ceased but lately and that it was the sudden cessation which had disturbed him. The fire had fallen low, but still it threw out a deep red glow. As he looked, he started in spite of his usual calm demeanor.

There on the great high-backed carved oak chair by the right side of the fireplace sat an enormous rat, steadily glaring at him with baleful eyes. He made a motion to it as though to hunt it away, but it did not stir. Then he made the motion of throwing something. Still it did not stir, but showed its great white teeth angrily, and its cruel eyes shone in the lamplight with an added vindictiveness.

Malcolmson felt amazed, and seizing the poker from the hearth ran at it to kill it. Before, however, he could strike it, the rat, with a squeak that sounded like the concentration of hate, jumped upon the floor, and, running up the rope of the alarm bell, disappeared in the darkness beyond the range of the green-shaded lamp. Instantly, strange to say, the noisy scampering of the rats in the wainscot began again.

By this time Malcolmson's mind was quite off the problem; and as a shrill cock-crow outside told him of the approach of morning, he went to bed and to sleep.

He slept so sound that he was not even waked by Mrs. Dempster coming in to make up his room. It was only when she had tidied up the place and got his breakfast ready and tapped on the screen which closed in his bed that he woke. He was a little tired still after his night's hard work, but a strong cup of tea soon freshened him up and, taking his book, he went out for his morning walk, bringing with him a few sandwiches lest he should not care to return till dinnertime. He found a quiet walk between high elms some way outside the town, and here he spent the greater part of the day studying his Laplace.

That evening, the scampering of the rats began earlier; indeed it had been going on before his arrival, and only ceased whilst his presence by its freshness disturbed them. After dinner he sat by the fire for a while and had a smoke; and then, having cleared his table, began to work as before. Tonight the rats disturbed him more than they had done on the previous night. How they scampered up and down and under and over! How they squeaked, and scratched, and gnawed! How they, getting bolder by degrees, came to the mouths of their holes and to the chinks and cracks and crannies in the wainscoting till their eyes shone like tiny lamps as the firelight rose and fell. But to him, now doubtless accustomed to them, their eyes were not wicked; only their playfulness touched him. Sometimes the boldest of them made sallies out on the floor or along the mouldings of the wainscot. Now and again as they disturbed him, Malcolmson made a sound to frighten them, smiting the table with his hand or giving a fierce "Hsh, hsh," so that they fled straightway to their holes.

And so the early part of the night wore on; and despite the noise Malcolmson got more and more immersed in his work.

All at once he stopped, as on the previous night, being overcome by a sudden sense of silence. There was not the faintest sound of gnaw, or scratch, or squeak. The silence was as of the grave. He remembered the odd occurrence of the previous night, and instinctively he looked at the chair standing close by the fireside. And then a very odd sensation thrilled through him.

There, on the great old high-backed carved oak chair beside the fireplace sat the same enormous rat, steadily glaring at him with baleful eyes.

Instinctively, he took the nearest thing to his hand, a book of logarithms, and flung it at it. The book was badly aimed, and the rat did not stir, so again the poker performance of the previous night was repeated; and again the rat, being closely pursued, fled up the rope of the alarm bell. Strangely too, the departure of this rat was instantly followed by the renewal of the noise made by the general rat community. On this occasion, as on the previous one, Malcolmson could not see at what part of the room the rat disappeared, for the green shade of his lamp left the upper part of the room in darkness, and the fire had burned low.

On looking at his watch, he found it was close on midnight; and, not sorry for the diversion, he made up his fire and made himself his nightly pot of tea. He began to think that he would like to know where the rat disappeared to, for he had certain ideas for the morrow not entirely disconnected with a rat-trap. Accordingly, he lit another lamp and placed it so that it would shine well into the right-hand corner of the wall by the fireplace. Then he got all the books he had with him and placed them handy to throw at the vermin. Finally, he lifted the rope of the alarm bell and placed the end of it on the table, fixing the extreme end under the lamp. As he handled it he could not help noticing how pliable it was, especially for so strong a rope, and one not in use. "You could hang a man with it," he thought to himself. When his preparations were made he looked around, and said complacently:

"There now, my friend, I think we shall learn something of you this time!" He began his work again, and though as before somewhat disturbed at first by the noise of the rats, soon lost himself in his propositions and problems.

Again he was called to his immediate surroundings suddenly. This time it might not have been the sudden silence only which took his attention; there was a slight movement of the rope, and the lamp moved. Without stirring, he looked to see if his pile of books was within range, and then cast his eye along the rope. As he looked, he saw the great rat drop from the rope on the oak armchair and sit there glaring at him. He raised a book in his right hand, and taking careful aim, flung it at the rat. The latter, with a quick movement, sprang aside and dodged the missile. He then took another book, and a third, and flung them one after another at the rat, but each time unsuccessfully. At last, as he stood with a book poised in his hand to throw, the rat squeaked and seemed afraid. This made Malcolmson more than ever eager to strike, and the book flew and struck the rat a resounding blow. It gave a terrified squeak, and turning on his pursuer a look of terrible malevolence, ran up the chair-back and made a great jump to the rope of the alarm bell and ran up it like lightning. The lamp rocked under the sudden strain, but it was a heavy one and did not topple over. Malcolmson kept his eyes on the rat, and saw it by the light of the second lamp leap to a moulding of the wainscot and disappear through a hole in one of the great pictures which hung on the wall, obscured and invisible through its coating of dirt and dust.

"I shall look up my friend's habitation in the morning," said the student, as he went over to collect his books. "The third picture from the fireplace; I shall not forget." He picked up the books one by one, commenting on them as he lifted them. "*Conic Sections* he does not mind, nor *Cycloidal Oscillations*, nor the *Principia*, nor *Quaternions*, nor *Thermodynamics*. Now for the book that fetched him!" Malcolmson took it up and looked at it. As he did so he started, a sudden pallor overspread his face. He looked round uneasily and shivered slightly, as he murmured to himself:

"The Bible my mother gave me! What an odd coincidence." He sat down to work again, and the rats in the wainscot renewed their gambols. They did not disturb him, however; somehow their presence gave him a sense of companionship. He went to bed as the first streak of dawn stole in through the eastern window.

He slept heavily but uneasily and dreamed much; and when Mrs. Dempster woke him late in the morning he seemed ill at ease, and for a few minutes did not seem to realise exactly where he was. His first request rather surprised the servant.

"Mrs. Dempster, when I am out today I wish you would get the steps and dust or wash those pictures—especially that one the third from the fireplace—I want to see what they are."

He paid a visit to Mrs. Witham at "The Good Traveller." He found a stranger in the cosy sitting-room with the landlady, who was introduced to him as Dr. Thornhill. She was not quite at ease, and this, combined with the doctor's plunging at once into a series of questions, made Malcolmson come to the conclusion that his presence was not an accident, so without preliminary he said:

"Did Mrs. Witham ask you to come here and see me and advise me?"

Dr. Thornhill for a moment was taken aback, and Mrs. Witham got fiery red and turned away; but the doctor was a frank and ready man, and he answered at once and openly.

"She did: but she didn't intend you to know it. She told me that she did not like he idea of your being in that house all by yourself, and that she thought you took too much strong tea. In fact, she wants me to advise you if possible to give up the tea and the very late hours."

Malcolmson with a bright smile held out his hand. "I promise to take no more strong tea—no tea at all till you let me—and I shall go to bed tonight at one o'clock at latest. Will that do?"

"Capital," said the doctor. "Now tell us all that you noticed in the old house," and so Malcolmson then and there told in minute detail all that had happened in the last two nights. He was interrupted every now and then by some exclamation from Mrs. Witham, till finally when he told of the episode of the Bible the landlady's pent-up emotions found vent in a shriek; and it was not till a stiff glass of brandy and water had been administered that she grew composed again. Dr. Thornhill listened with a face of growing gravity, and when the narrative was complete and Mrs. Witham had been restored, he asked:

"The rat always went up the rope of the alarm bell?"

"Always."

"I suppose you know," said the doctor after a pause, "what the rope is?"

"No!"

"It is," said the doctor slowly, "the very rope which the hangman used for all the victims of the Judge's judicial rancour!" Here he was interrupted by another scream from Mrs. Witham, and steps had to be taken for her recovery. Malcolmson having looked at his watch and found that it was close to his dinner hour, had gone home before her complete recovery.

When Malcolmson arrived home he found that it was a little after his usual time, and Mrs. Dempster had gone away. The evening was colder than might have been expected in April, and a heavy wind was blowing with such rapidly increasing strength that there was every promise of a storm during the night. For a few minutes after his entrance, the noise of the rats ceased; but so soon as they became accustomed to his presence they began again. He was glad to hear them, for he felt once more the feeling of companionship in their noise, and his mind ran back to the strange fact that they only ceased to manifest themselves when that other—the great rat with the baleful eyes—came upon the scene. Malcolmson sat down to his dinner with a good appetite and a buoyant spirit. After his dinner and a cigarette he sat steadily down to work, determined not to let anything disturb him, for he remembered his promise to the doctor, and made up his mind to make the best of the time at his disposal.

For an hour or so he worked all right, and then his thoughts began to wander from his books. The actual circumstances around him, the calls on his physical attention, and his nervous susceptibility were not to be denied. By this time the wind had become a gale, and the gale a storm. The old house, solid though it was, seemed to shake to its foundations, and the storm roared and raged through its many chimneys and its queer old gables, producing strange, unearthly sounds in the empty rooms and corridors. Even the great alarm bell on the roof must have felt the force of the wind, for the rope rose and fell slightly, as though the bell were moved a little from time to time, and the limber rope fell on the oak floor with a hard and hollow sound.

As Malcolmson listened to it he bethought himself of the doctor's words, "It is the rope which the hangman used for the victims of the Judge's judicial rancour," and he went over to the corner of the fireplace and took it in his hand to look at it. There seemed a sort of deadly interest in it, and as he stood there he lost himself for a moment in speculation as to who these victims were, and the grim wish of the Judge to have such a ghastly relic ever under his eyes. As he stood there, the swaying of the bell on the roof still lifted the rope now and again; but presently there came a new sensation—a sort of tremor in the rope, as though something was moving along it.

Looking up instinctively, Malcolmson saw the great rat coming slowly down toward him, glaring at him steadily. He dropped the rope and started back with a muttered curse, and the rat, turning, ran up the rope again and disappeared, and at the same instant Malcolmson became conscious that the noise of the rats, which had ceased for a while, began again.

All this set him thinking, and it occurred to him that he had not investigated the lair of the rat nor looked at the pictures, as he had intended. He lit the other lamp without the shade, and, holding it up, went and stood opposite the third picture from the fireplace on the right-hand side where he had seen the rat disappear on the previous night.

At the first glance he started back so suddenly that he almost dropped the lamp, and a deadly pallor spread over his face. His knees shook, and heavy drops of sweat came on his forehead, and he trembled like an aspen. But he was young and plucky, and pulled himself together, and after the pause of a few seconds stepped forward again, raised the lamp, and examined the picture which had been dusted and washed, and now stood out clearly.

It was of a judge dressed in his robes of scarlet and ermine. His face was strong and merciless, evil, crafty, and vindictive, with a sensual mouth, hooked nose of ruddy colour, and shaped like the beak of a bird of prey. The rest of the face was of a cadaverous colour. The eyes were of peculiar brilliance and with a terribly malignant expression. As he looked at them, Malcolmson grew cold, for he saw there the very counterpart of the eyes of the great rat. The lamp almost fell from his hand, for he saw the rat with its baleful eyes peering out through the hole in the corner of the picture, and noted the sudden cessation of the noise of the other rats. However, he pulled himself together, and went on with his examination of the picture.

The Judge was seated in a great high-backed carved oak chair, on the right-hand side of a great stone fireplace where, in the corner, a rope hung down from the ceiling, its end lying coiled on the floor. With a feeling of something like horror, Malcolmson recognised the scene of the room as it stood, and gazed around him in an awestruck manner as though he expected to find some strange presence behind him. Then he looked over to the corner of the fire-place—and with a loud cry, he let the lamp fall from his hand.

There, in the Judge's arm-chair, with the rope hanging behind, sat the rat with the Judge's baleful eyes, now intensified and with a fiendish leer. Save for the howling of the storm without, there was silence.

"This will not do," he said to himself. "If I go on like this I shall become a crazy fool. This must stop! I promised the doctor I would not take tea. Faith, he was pretty right! My nerves must have been getting into a queer state. Funny I did not notice it. I never felt better in my life. However, it is all right now, and I shall not be such a fool again."

Then he mixed himself a good stiff glass of brandy and water and resolutely sat down to his work.

It was nearly an hour when he looked up from his book, disturbed by the sudden stillness. Without, the wind howled and roared louder than ever, and the rain drove in sheets against the windows, beating like hail on the glass; but within there was no sound whatever save the echo of the wind as it roared in the great chimney and now and then a hiss as a few raindrops found their way down the chimney in a lull of the storm. The fire had fallen low and had ceased to flame, though it threw out a red glow. Malcolmson listened attentively and presently heard a thin, squeaking noise, very faint. It came from the corner of the room where the rope hung down, and he thought it was the creaking of the rope on the floor as the swaying of the bell raised and lowered it. Looking up, however, he saw in the dim light the great rat clinging to the rope and gnawing it. The rope was already nearly gnawed through—he could see the lighter colour where the strands were laid bare. As he looked, the job was completed, and the severed end of the rope fell clattering on the oaken floor, whilst for an instant the great rat remained like a knob or tassel at the end of the rope, which now began to sway to and fro. Malcolmson felt for a moment another pang of terror as he thought that now the possibility of calling the outer world to his assistance was cut off, but an intense anger took its place, and seizing the book he was reading he hurled it at the rat. The blow was well aimed, but before the missile could reach him, the rat dropped off and struck the floor with a soft thud. Malcolmson instantly rushed over toward the rat, but it darted away and disappeared in the darkness of the shadows of the room. Malcolmson felt that his work was over for the night, and determined then and there to vary the monotony of the proceedings by a hunt for the rat, and took off the green shade of the lamp so as to ensure a wider spreading light. As he did so, the gloom of the upper part of the room was relieved, and in the new flood of light, great by comparison with the previous darkness, the pictures on the wall stood out boldly. From where he stood, Malcolmson saw right opposite to him the third picture on the wall from the right of the fireplace. He rubbed his eyes in surprise, and then a great fear began to come upon him.

In the centre of the picture was a great irregular patch of brown canvas, as fresh as when it was stretched on the frame. The background was as before, with chair and chimney-corner and rope, but the figure of the Judge had disappeared.

Malcolmson, almost in a chill of horror, turned slowly round, and then he began to shake and tremble like a man in a palsy. His strength seemed to have left him, and he was incapable of action or movement, hardly even of thought. He could only see and hear.

There, on the great high-backed carved oak chair, sat the Judge in his robes of scarlet and ermine, with his baleful eyes glaring vindictively, and a smile of triumph on the resolute, cruel mouth, as he lifted with his hands a black cap. Malcolmson felt as if the blood was running from his heart, as one does in moments of prolonged suspense. There was a singing in his ears. Without, he could hear the roar and howl of the tempest, and through it, swept on the storm, came the striking of midnight by the great chimes in the marketplace. He stood for a space of time that seemed to him endless still as a statue, and with wide-open, horror-struck eyes, breathless. As the clock struck, so the smile of triumph on the Judge's face intensified, and at the last stroke of midnight, he placed the black cap on his head.

Slowly and deliberately, the Judge rose from his chair and picked up the piece of the rope of the alarm bell which lay on the floor, drew it through his hands as if he enjoyed its touch, and then deliberately began to knot one end of it, fashioning it into a noose. This he tightened and tested with his foot, pulling hard at it till he was satisfied and then making a running noose of it, which he held in his hand. Then he began to move along the table on the opposite side toward Malcolmson, keeping his eyes on him until he had passed him, when with a quick movement he stood in front of the door. Malcolmson then began to feel that he was trapped, and tried to think of what he should do. There was some fascination in the Judge's eyes, which he never took off him, and he had, perforce, to look. He saw the Judge approach—still keeping between him and the door—and raise the noose and throw it toward him as if to entangle him. With a great effort, he made a quick movement to one side, and saw the rope fall beside him, and heard it strike the oaken floor. Again the Judge raised the noose and tried to ensnare him, ever keeping his baleful eyes fixed on him, and each time by a mighty effort the student just managed to evade it. So this went on for many times, the Judge seeming never discouraged nor discomposed at failure, but playing as a cat does with a mouse. At last, in despair, which had reached its climax, Malcolmson cast a quick glance round him. The lamp seemed to have blazed up, and there was a fairly good light in the room. At the many rat-holes and in the chinks and crannies of the wainscot he saw the rats' eyes; and this aspect, that was purely physical, gave him a gleam of comfort. He looked around and saw that the rope of the great alarm bell was laden with rats. Every inch of it was covered with them; and more and more were pouring through the small circular hole in the ceiling whence it emerged, so that with their weight the bell was beginning to sway.

Hark! it had swayed till the clapper had touched the bell. The sound was but a tiny one, but the bell was only beginning to sway, and it would increase.

At the sound the Judge, who had been keeping his eyes fixed on Malcolmson, looked up, and a scowl of diabolical anger overspread his face. His eyes fairly glowed like hot coals, and he stamped his foot with a sound that seemed to make the house shake. A dreadful peal of thunder broke overhead as he raised the rope again, whilst the rats kept running up and down the rope as though working against time. This time, instead of throwing it, he drew close to his victim and held open the noose as he approached. As he came closer there seemed something paralysing in his very presence, and Malcolmson stood rigid as a corpse. He felt the Judge's icy fingers touch his throat as he adjusted the rope. The noose tightened—tightened. Then the Judge, taking the rigid form of the student in his arms, carried him over and placed him standing in the oak chair, and stepping up beside him, put his hand up and caught the end of the swaying rope of the alarm bell. As he raised his hand the rats fled squeaking and disappeared through the hole in the ceiling. Taking the end of the noose which was round Malcolmson's neck he tied it to the hanging-bell rope, and then descending pulled away the chair.

When the alarm bell of the Judge's House began to sound, a crowd soon assembled. Lights and torches of various kinds appeared, and soon a silent crowd was hurrying to the spot. They knocked loudly at the door, but there was no reply. Then they burst in the door and poured into the great dining-room the doctor at the head.

There, at the end of the rope of the great alarm bell, hung the body of the student, and on the face of the Judge in the picture was a malignant smile.

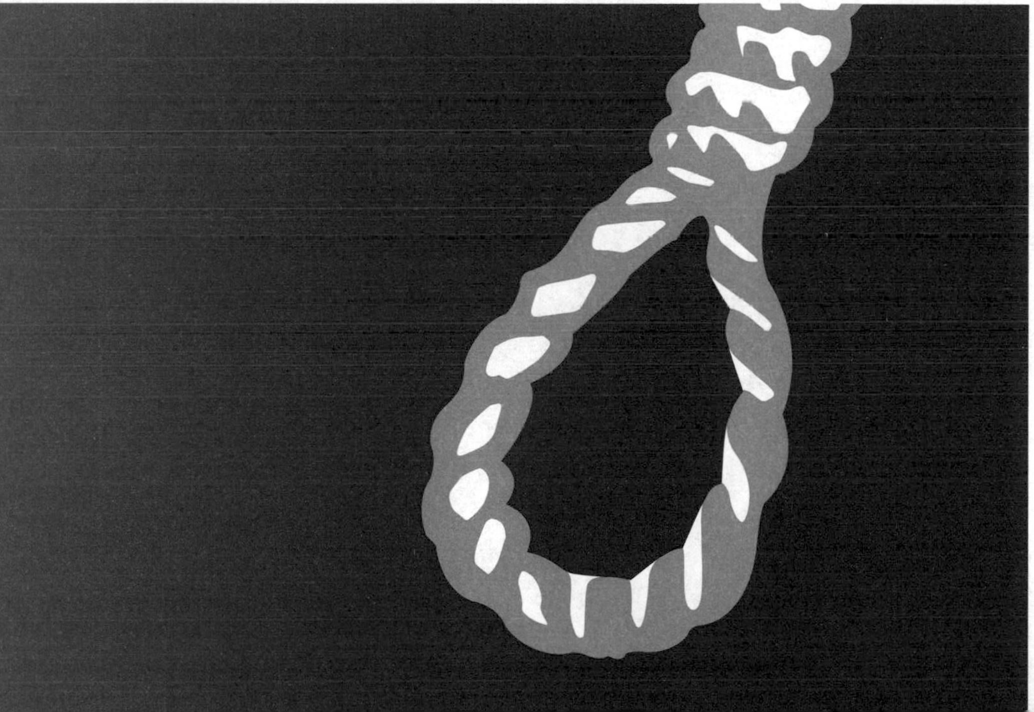

The Best Scary Movies for the Whole Family

Frankenstein (1931)—*the black-and-white classic with Boris Karloff as the Monster*

Bride of Frankenstein (1935)—*the sequel to the 1931* Frankenstein, *which compares favorably to the original*

Young Frankenstein (1974)—*one of the great movie satires of all time, from Mel Brooks and Gene Wilder, with Wilder as Dr. Fredrick Frankenstein and Peter Boyle as the Monster*

Dracula (1931)—*the classic version with Bela Lugosi, in his greatest role, as Count Dracula*

The Wolf Man (1941)—*the classic werewolf movie, with Claude Rains, Bela Lugosi, and Lon Chaney Jr. as the Wolf Man*

The Mummy (1999)—*the best of all the B-movie mummy tales, with great special effects and some good laughs, with Brendan Fraser and Rachel Weisz*

The Thing from Outer Space (1951)—*a 1950s paranoid classic, based on the novella, "Who Goes There?" by John W. Campbell, and inspiring John Carpenter's 1982 version,* The Thing *(The 1951 film is not yet available on VHS or DVD, but look for it on TV, as it occasionally turns up on cable or local channels.)*

Invasion of the Body Snatchers (1956)—*another 1950s paranoid classic, this time with a full-fledged "alien" invasion—re-made twice, in 1978 with Donald Sutherland and in 1993 with Gabrielle Anwar*

The Pit and the Pendulum (1961)—*based on the Poe classic, with Vincent Price and directed by Roger Corman*

The Haunting (1963)—*based on Shirley Jackson's novel* The Haunting of Hill House

The Adventures of Ichabod and Mr. Toad (1949)—*two Disney animated TV films, "The Wind in the Willows" and the wonderful Headless Horseman classic, "The Legend of Sleepy Hollow"*

Monsters, Inc. (2001)—*the computer-animated movie from Pixar, much more funny than scary, and perfect for young children*

All-time Halloween Family Classic

It's the Great Pumpkin, Charlie Brown (1966)—*the animated* Peanuts *TV Halloween special*

caw
caw
caw
The Scarecrow

5
caw
a folk tale
hear...

caw
caw
caw
caw
caw
caw

track
3

Horace and John lived with their aged father, Silas, on a broken-down farm in the hills. It was a hard living, but the two brothers had always been too lazy for the work. They liked to play cards and drink whiskey, though neither was smart enough to be any good at cards, and John couldn't hold his liquor.

Silas was too old to work the farm like he used to, and he complained that his sons were more interested in playing games and getting drunk than in keeping a roof over their heads. When the boys got tired of their father's nagging, they made him live in a shed behind the house. There was no heat, and Silas had to share his home with the chickens. They mistreated him terribly, but Silas was too feeble to fight back.

One night, after the boys had been drinking, Silas demanded, "How can you treat your own father this way, forcing me to sleep with chickens while you two carry on?"

"Be grateful we let you stay here at all, old man," said Horace.

"You're no sons of mine," Silas spat. John pushed him to the floor and laughed.

Silas sulked away to go sleep in the chicken coop.

Later that night, John visited the outhouse. On his way back to bed, he stopped by the chicken shack to have a smoke. He flicked his still-lit cigarette butt toward his father's shed and walked back to the house to sleep.

The next morning, all they found of the shed was a smoldering frame. It had burnt down in the night with Silas in it. The fire had consumed Silas, burning away all of his skin. The boys simply buried what was left of their father in a shallow grave.

It was several weeks later when John got the idea to make a scarecrow. Horace and John found it unbearably dull on the farm all alone with no one to taunt or abuse. As John and Horace stared into the orange flames dancing in the hearth, John lit on the idea. "We could make a doll the size of a man. It would be fun and we could put it in the garden to scare away the birds and the rabbits."

"And we could name it 'Silas,'" said Horace, a wicked smile forming on his face.

The boys made the scarecrow from straw and old rags. They dressed it in Silas's old overalls, his favorite red shirt, and his tattered straw hat. They sewed on a sad-looking mouth and a crooked nose, with two shiny black buttons for his eyes.

Every day they hung Silas from a pole in the garden, under the beating sun. Each night the boys would bring him inside so that he wouldn't get ruined if it rained. Sometimes, they would talk to him. "Hot enough for you today, Silas?" one of them might say. Then the other, imitating the voice of their dead father, would answer, "I'm *dyying* out there, son!" They both laughed a long time at that one. But not Silas.

When things went badly as they often did since neither Horace nor John liked to work much—they took it out on Silas. They would curse him as they passed him in the field, or even kick or punch him as he sat in the corner of the house. Sometimes, when they were drinking, they would ask Silas, "Want something to drink?" and then spit whiskey in his face.

One night, after John had kicked Silas as he sat by the fire, he thought he heard Silas grunt.

"Did you hear that?" he asked Horace.

"Hear what?" Horace said.

"It was Silas; he grunted."

"You're drunk," Horace said and laughed at John.

The next night, John was still certain that Silas had grunted and was afraid. "I swear his eyes were following me all day," he said.

"You've been out in the sun too long," said Horace.

The two played cards that night with Silas sitting in the corner. When John turned around, he saw that Silas was now sitting by the fire. "He's moved!" John gasped. "He was in the corner and now he's in front of the hearth—"

Horace cut him off, "Don't be foolish. You probably just don't remember moving him." Then Horace had an idea. "Let's deal Silas in the next hand. It'll be more fun with three players." John was still frightened of the scarecrow, but did not say anything to Horace. All night, they played hand after hand with Silas. Each time, Horace would tease the doll, "You lose again, Silas."

After a few glasses of whiskey, John joined in. When Horace got up to get another bottle, John taunted Silas, "You're not very good at cards, are you, Silas? You're not really good for much, are you?" Just then, the scarecrow's black eyes seemed to come alive, and he leaped across the table at John, wrapping his straw hands around John's scrawny neck. John screamed and fell to the floor.

"What are you doing?!" Horace looked at John as if he were crazy.

"He—he…Silas came at me. He tried to strangle me!" screamed John.

Horace just shook his head and laughed. "Look," he said, picking Silas up by the collar and shaking his limp body. "He's just a scarecrow." John was wide-eyed and trembling. "Aw, you never could hold your whiskey," said Horace.

The next morning, the boys forgot to bring Silas out to the garden. Horace called to his brother. "John! Bring out Silas, so the rabbits don't eat the rest of our vegetables." John was afraid of the scarecrow, but he did not want his brother to think him a fool. So he trudged up to the house to fetch Silas.

An hour passed, but John did not return. "What on earth could be taking him so long?" Horace grumbled. He walked over to the house and opened the door. He called for his brother but heard no reply. As he walked toward the table, he slipped in a pool of liquid, fell, and hit his head. Dazed and lying on the floor, he saw that the puddle was red, and it felt thick and sticky. Under the table lay his brother John, dead and staring in horror, the flesh removed from every inch of his corpse. Just then, Horace looked up and saw the figure of Silas standing over him, a large kitchen knife in his hand. Silas was smiling with the crooked mouth and black-button eyes they had sewn on him, wearing the freshly harvested skin of Horace's brother.

The Best Scary Movies Just for Adults

Psycho (1960)—*Alfred Hitchcock's classic movie about a boy and his mother that started the slasher movie genre, with Anthony Perkins and Janet Leigh*

Halloween (1978)—*John Carpenter's brilliant psycho-killer classic that started the trend of movies about relentless killers who just won't die, with Jamie Lee Curtis*

Night of the Living Dead (1968)—*George Romero's low-budget classic about zombies who eat human flesh*

The Shining (1980)—*Stanley Kubrick's loose adaptation of the Stephen King novel, with Jack Nicholson as a slowly unravelling lunatic in an isolated, snowbound retreat*

Poltergeist (1982)—*the scariest haunted house story yet, with two valuable lessons: don't build your house on an old Indian burial ground, and kids shouldn't watch too much TV*

A Nightmare on Elm Street (1984)—*Freddy Krueger just won't get out of those teenagers' dreams and kills them in creatively sadistic ways. If this doesn't turn you to coffee, nothing will*

Bram Stoker's Dracula (1992)—*Francis Ford Coppola's beautifully filmed, campy, and oddly romantic version of Stoker's classic novel, with Anthony Hopkins, Winona Ryder, and Gary Oldman as Count "Vlad"*

Scream (1996)—*from director Wes Craven, this is probably the funnest of all the really scary movies, a horrifying slasher movie with a real sense of humor about itself*

The Sixth Sense (1999)—*the creepy, suspenseful tale of a boy who can see ghosts, with Bruce Willis and Haley Joel Osment*

The Blair Witch Project (1999)—*filmed in grainy, black-and-white film and shaky, seasick-inducing videotape, the basic message of this movie is: stay out of the woods*

The Others (2001)—*a throwback to old-fashioned storytelling, a slowly building, suspenseful ghost story with a twist, with Nicole Kidman*

The Ring (2002)—*a truly terrifying movie about watching...a killer videotape*

All-Time Scariest Movie Ever

The Exorcist (1973)—*the pea-soup-spewing tale of a little girl's possession by Satan, not for the faint of heart, with Linda Blair and Max von Sydow*

6

The Signal-Man

by Charles Dickens

alloa! Below there!”

When he heard a voice thus calling to him, he was standing at the door of his box with a flag in his hand, furled round its short pole. One would have thought, considering the nature of the ground, that he could not have doubted from what quarter the voice came; but instead of looking up to where I stood on the top of the steep cutting nearly over his head, he turned himself about, and looked down the Line. There was something remarkable in his manner of doing so, though I could not have said for my life what. But I know it was remarkable enough to attract my notice, even though his figure was foreshortened and shadowed, down in the deep trench, and mine was high above him, so steeped in the glow of an angry sunset, that I had shaded my eyes with my hand before I saw him at all.

“Halloa! Below!”

From looking down the Line, he turned himself about again, and, raising his eyes, saw my figure high above him.

“Is there any path by which I can come down and speak to you?”

He looked up at me without replying, and I looked down at him without pressing him too soon with a repetition of my idle question.

Just then there came a vague vibration in the earth and air, quickly changing into a violent pulsation, and an oncoming rush that caused me to start back, as though it had force to draw me down. When such vapour as rose to my height from this rapid train had passed me, and was skimming away over the landscape, I looked down again, and saw him refurling the flag he had shown while the train went by.

I repeated my inquiry. After a pause, during which he seemed to regard me with fixed attention, he motioned with his rolled-up flag towards a point on my level, some two or three hundred yards distant. I called down to him, "All right!" and made for that point. There, by dint of looking closely about me, I found a rough zigzag descending path notched out, which I followed.

The cutting was extremely deep, and unusually precipitate. It was made through a clammy stone, that became oozier and wetter as I went down. For these reasons, I found the way long enough to give me time to recall a singular air of reluctance or compulsion with which he had pointed out the path.

When I came down low enough upon the zigzag descent to see him again, I saw that he was standing between the rails on the way by which the train had lately passed, in an attitude as if he were waiting for me to appear. He had his left hand at his chin, and that left elbow rested on his right hand, crossed over his breast. His attitude was one of such expectation and watchfulness that I stopped a moment, wondering at it.

I resumed my downward way, and stepping out upon the level of the railroad, and drawing nearer to him, saw that he was a dark sallow man, with a dark beard and rather heavy eyebrows. His post was in as solitary and dismal a place as ever I saw. On either side, a dripping-wet wall of jagged stone, excluding all view but a strip of sky; the perspective one way only a crooked prolongation of this great dungeon; the shorter perspective in the other direction terminating in a gloomy red light, and the gloomier entrance to a black tunnel, in whose massive architecture there was a barbarous, depressing, and forbidding air. So little sunlight ever found its way to this spot, that it had an earthy, deadly smell; and so much cold wind rushed through it, that it struck chill to me, as if I had left the natural world.

Before he stirred, I was near enough to him to have touched him. Not even then removing his eyes from mine, he stepped back one step, and lifted his hand.

This was a lonesome post to occupy (I said), and it had riveted my attention when I looked down from up yonder. A visitor was a rarity, I should suppose; not an unwelcome rarity, I hoped? In me, he merely saw a man who had been shut up within narrow limits all his life, and who, being at last set free, had a newly-awakened interest in these great works. To such purpose I spoke to him; but I am far from sure of the terms I used; for, besides that I am not happy in opening any conversation, there was something in the man that daunted me.

He directed a most curious look towards the red light near the tunnel's mouth, and looked all about it, as if something were missing from it, and then looked it me.

That light was part of his charge? Was it not?

He answered in a low voice,—"Don't you know it is?"

The monstrous thought came into my mind, as I perused the fixed eyes and the saturnine face, that this was a spirit, not a man. I have speculated since, whether there may have been infection in his mind.

In my turn, I stepped back. But in making the action, I detected in his eyes some latent fear of me. This put the monstrous thought to flight.

"You look at me," I said, forcing a smile, "as if you had a dread of me."

"I was doubtful," he returned, "whether I had seen you before."

"Where?"

He pointed to the red light he had looked at.

"There?" I said.

Intently watchful of me, he replied (but without sound), "Yes."

"My good fellow, what should I do there? However, be that as it may, I never was there, you may swear."

"I think I may," he rejoined. "Yes; I am sure I may."

His manner cleared, like my own. He replied to my remarks with readiness, and in well-chosen words. Had he much to do there? Yes; that was to say, he had enough responsibility to bear; but exactness and watchfulness were what was required of him, and of actual work—manual labour—he had next to none. To change that signal, to trim those lights, and to turn this iron handle now and then, was all he had to do under that head. Regarding those many long and lonely hours of which I seemed to make so much, he could only say that the routine of his life had shaped itself into that form, and he had grown used to it. He had taught himself a language down here,—if only to know it by sight, and to have formed his own crude ideas of its pronunciation, could be called learning it. He had also worked at fractions and decimals, and tried a little algebra; but he was, and had been as a boy, a poor hand at figures. Was it necessary for him when on duty always to remain in that channel of damp air, and could he never rise into the sunshine from between those high stone walls? Why, that depended upon times and circumstances. Under some conditions there would be less upon the Line than under others, and the same held good as to certain hours of the day and night. In bright weather, he did choose occasions for getting a little above these lower shadows; but, being at all times liable to be called by his electric bell, and at such times listening for it with redoubled anxiety, the relief was less than I would suppose.

He took me into his box, where there was a fire, a desk for an official book in which he had to make certain entries, a telegraphic instrument with its dial, face, and needles, and the little bell of which he had spoken. On my trusting that he would excuse the remark that he had been well educated, and (I hoped I might say without offence) perhaps educated above that station, he observed that instances of slight incongruity in such wise would rarely be found wanting among large bodies of men; that he had heard it was so in workhouses, in the police force, even in that last desperate resource, the army; and that he knew it was so, more or less, in any great railway staff. He had been, when young (if I could believe it, sitting in that hut,—he scarcely could), a student of natural philosophy, and had attended lectures; but he had run wild, misused his opportunities, gone down, and never risen again. He had no complaint to offer about that. He had made his bed, and he lay upon it. It was far too late to make another.

All that I have here condensed he said in a quiet manner, with his grave dark regards divided between me and the fire. He threw in the word, "Sir," from time to time, and especially when he referred to his youth,—as though to request me to understand that he claimed to be nothing but what I found him. He was several times interrupted by the little bell, and had to read off messages, and send replies. Once he had to stand without the door, and display a flag as a train passed, and make some verbal communication to the driver. In the discharge of his duties, I observed him to be remarkably exact and vigilant, breaking off his discourse at a syllable, and remaining silent until what he had to do was done.

In a word, I should have set this man down as one of the safest of men to be employed in that capacity, but for the circumstance that while he was speaking to me he twice broke off with a fallen colour, turned his face towards the little bell when it did NOT ring, opened the door of the hut (which was kept shut to exclude the unhealthy damp), and looked out towards the red light near the mouth of the tunnel. On both of those occasions, he came back to the fire with the inexplicable air upon him which I had remarked, without being able to define, when we were so far asunder.

Said I, when I rose to leave him, "You almost make me think that I have met with a contented man."

(I am afraid I must acknowledge that I said it to lead him on.)

"I believe I used to be so," he rejoined, in the low voice in which he had first spoken; "but I am troubled, sir, I am troubled."

He would have recalled the words if he could. He had said them, however, and I took them up quickly.

"With what? What is your trouble?"

"It is very difficult to impart, sir. It is very, very difficult to speak of. If ever you make me another visit, I will try to tell you."

"But I expressly intend to make you another visit. Say, when shall it be?"

"I go off early in the morning, and I shall be on again at ten to-morrow night, sir."

"I will come at eleven."

He thanked me, and went out at the door with me. "I'll show my white light, sir," he said, in his peculiar low voice, "till you have found the way up. When you have found it, don't call out! And when you are at the top, don't call out!"

His manner seemed to make the place strike colder to me, but I said no more than, "Very well."

"And when you come down tomorrow night, don't call out! Let me ask you a parting question. What made you cry, 'Halloa! Below there!' tonight?"

"Heaven knows," said I. "I cried something to that effect—"

"Not to that effect, sir. Those were the very words. I know them well."

"Admit those were the very words. I said them, no doubt, because I saw you below."

"For no other reason?"

"What other reason could I possibly have?"

"You had no feeling that they were conveyed to you in any supernatural way?"

"No."

He wished me good night, and held up his light. I walked by the side of the down Line of rails (with a very disagreeable sensation of a train coming behind me) until I found the path. It was easier to mount than to descend, and I got back to my inn without any adventure.

Punctual to my appointment, I placed my foot on the first notch of the zigzag next night, as the distant clocks were striking eleven. He was waiting for me at the bottom, with his white light on. "I have not called out," I said, when we came close together; "may I speak now?" "By all means, sir." "Good night, then, and here's my hand." "Good night, sir, and here's mine." With that we walked side by side to his box, entered it, closed the door, and sat down by the fire.

"I have made up my mind, sir," he began, bending forward as soon as we were seated, and speaking in a tone but a little above a whisper, "that you shall not have to ask me twice what troubles me. I took you for someone else yesterday evening. That troubles me."

"That mistake?"

"No. That someone else."

"Who is it?"

"I don't know."

"Like me?"

"I don't know. I never saw the face. The left arm is across the face, and the right arm is waved,—violently waved. This way."

I followed his action with my eyes, and it was the action of an arm gesticulating, with the utmost passion and vehemence, "For God's sake, clear the way!"

"One moonlight night," said the man, "I was sitting here, when I heard a voice cry, 'Halloa! Below there!' I started up, looked from that door, and saw this someone else standing by the red light near the tunnel, waving as I just now showed you. The voice seemed hoarse with shouting, and it cried, 'Look out! Look out!' And then again, 'Halloa! Below there! Look out!' I caught up my lamp, turned it on red, and ran towards the figure, calling, 'What's wrong? What has happened? Where?' It stood just outside the blackness of the tunnel. I advanced so close upon it that I wondered at its keeping the sleeve across its eyes. I ran right up at it and had my hand stretched out to pull the sleeve away, when it was gone."

"Into the tunnel?" said I.

"No. I ran on into the tunnel, five hundred yards. I stopped, and held my lamp above my head, and saw the figures of the measured distance, and saw the wet stains stealing down the walls and trickling through the arch. I ran out again faster than I had run in (for I had a mortal abhorrence of the place upon me), and I looked all round the red light with my own red light, and I went up the iron ladder to the gallery atop of it, and I came down again, and ran back here. I telegraphed both ways, 'An alarm has been given. Is anything wrong?' The answer came back, both ways, 'All well.'"

Resisting the slow touch of a frozen finger tracing out my spine, I showed him how this figure must be a deception of his sense of sight; and how figures, originating in disease of the delicate nerves that minister to the functions of the eye, were known to have often troubled patients, some of whom had become conscious of the nature of their affliction, and had even proved it by experiments upon themselves. "As to an imaginary cry," said I, "do but listen for a moment to the wind in this unnatural valley while we speak so low, and to the wild harp it makes of the telegraph wires."

That was all very well, he returned, after we had sat listening for a while, and he ought to know something of the wind and the wires,—he who so often passed long winter nights there, alone and watching. But he would beg to remark that he had not finished.

I asked his pardon, and he slowly added these words, touching my arm,—

"Within six hours after the Appearance, the memorable accident on this Line happened, and within ten hours the dead and wounded were brought along through the tunnel over the spot where the figure had stood."

A disagreeable shudder crept over me, but I did my best against it. It was not to be denied, I rejoined, that this was a remarkable coincidence, calculated deeply to impress his mind. But it was unquestionable that remarkable coincidences did continually occur, and they must be taken into account in dealing with such a subject. Though to be sure I must admit, I added (for I thought I saw that he was going to bring the objection to bear upon me), men of common sense did not allow much for coincidences in making the ordinary calculations of life.

He again begged to remark that he had not finished.

I again begged his pardon for being betrayed into interruptions.

"This," he said, again laying his hand upon my arm, and glancing over his shoulder with hollow eyes, "was just a year ago. Six or seven months passed, and I had recovered from the surprise and shock, when one morning, as the day was breaking, I, standing at the door, looked towards the red light, and saw the spectre again." He stopped, with a fixed look at me.

"Did it cry out?"

"No. It was silent."

"Did it wave its arm?"

"No. It leaned against the shaft of the light, with both hands before the face. Like this."

Once more I followed his action with my eyes. It was an action of mourning. I have seen such an attitude in stone figures on tombs.

"Did you go up to it?"

"I came in and sat down, partly to collect my thoughts, partly because it had turned me faint. When I went to the door again, daylight was above me, and the ghost was gone."

"But nothing followed? Nothing came of this?"

He touched me on the arm with his forefinger twice or thrice giving a ghastly nod each time:—

"That very day, as a train came out of the tunnel, I noticed, at a carriage window on my side, what looked like a confusion of hands and heads, and something waved. I saw it just in time to signal the driver, Stop! He shut off, and put his brake on, but the train drifted past here a hundred and fifty yards or more. I ran after it, and, as I went along, heard terrible screams and cries. A beautiful young lady had died instantaneously in one of the compartments, and was brought in here, and laid down on this floor between us."

Involuntarily I pushed my chair back, as I looked from the boards at which he pointed to himself.

"True, sir. True. Precisely as it happened, so I tell it you."

I could think of nothing to say, to any purpose, and my mouth was very dry. The wind and the wires took up the story with a long lamenting wail.

He resumed. "Now, sir, mark this, and judge how my mind is troubled. The spectre came back a week ago. Ever since, it has been there, now and again, by fits and starts."

"At the light?"

"At the Danger-light."

"What does it seem to do?"

He repeated, if possible with increased passion and vehemence, that former gesticulation of, "For God's sake, clear the way!"

Then he went on. "I have no peace or rest for it. It calls to me, for many minutes together, in an agonised manner, 'Below there! Look out! Look out!' It stands waving to me. It rings my little bell—"

I caught at that. "Did it ring your bell yesterday evening when I was here, and you went to the door?"

"Twice."

"Why, see," said I, "how your imagination misleads you. My eyes were on the bell, and my ears were open to the bell, and if I am a living man, it did NOT ring at those times. No, nor at any other time, except when it was rung in the natural course of physical things by the station communicating with you."

He shook his head. "I have never made a mistake as to that yet, sir. I have never confused the spectre's ring with the man's. The ghost's ring is a strange vibration in the bell that it derives from nothing else, and I have not asserted that the bell stirs to the eye. I don't wonder that you failed to hear it. But I heard it."

"And did the spectre seem to be there, when you looked out?"

"It *was* there."

"Both times?"

He repeated firmly: "Both times."

"Will you come to the door with me, and look for it now?"

He bit his under lip as though he were somewhat unwilling, but arose. I opened the door, and stood on the step, while he stood in the doorway. There was the Danger-light. There was the dismal mouth of the tunnel. There were the high, wet stone walls of the cutting. There were the stars above them.

"Do you see it?" I asked him, taking particular note of his face. His eyes were prominent and strained, but not very much more so, perhaps, than my own had been when I had directed them earnestly towards the same spot.

"No," he answered. "It is not there."

"Agreed," said I.

We went in again, shut the door, and resumed our seats. I was thinking how best to improve this advantage, if it might be called one, when he took up the conversation in such a matter-of-course way, so assuming that there could be no serious question of fact between us, that I felt myself placed in the weakest of positions.

"By this time you will fully understand, sir," he said, "that what troubles me so dreadfully is the question, What does the spectre mean?"

I was not sure, I told him, that I did fully understand.

"What is its warning against?" he said, ruminating, with his eyes on the fire, and only by times turning them on me. "What is the danger? Where is the danger? There is danger overhanging somewhere on the Line. Some dreadful calamity will happen. It is not to be doubted this third time, after what has gone before. But surely this is a cruel haunting of me. What can I do?"

He pulled out his handkerchief and wiped the drops from his heated forehead.

"If I telegraph DANGER, on either side of me, or on both, I can give no reason for it," he went on, wiping the palms of his hands. "I should get into trouble, and do no good. They would think I was mad. This is the way it would work,—Message: DANGER! TAKE CARE! Answer: WHAT DANGER? WHERE? Message: DON'T KNOW. BUT, FOR GOD'S SAKE, TAKE CARE! They would displace me. What else could they do?"

His pain of mind was most pitiable to see. It was the mental torture of a conscientious man, oppressed beyond endurance by an unintelligible responsibility involving life.

"When it first stood under the Danger-light," he went on, putting his dark hair back from his head, and drawing his hands outward across and across his temples in an extremity of feverish distress, "why not tell me where that accident was to happen,—if it must happen? Why not tell me how it could be averted,—if it could have been averted? When on its second coming it hid its face, why not tell me, instead, 'She is going to die. Let them keep her at home'? If it came, on those two occasions, only to show me that its warnings were true, and so to prepare me for the third, why not warn me plainly now? And I, Lord help me! A mere poor signal-man on this solitary station! Why not go to somebody with credit to be believed, and power to act?"

When I saw him in this state, I saw that for the poor man's sake, as well as for the public safety, what I had to do for the time was to compose his mind. Therefore, setting aside all question of reality or unreality between us, I represented to him that whoever thoroughly discharged his duty must do well, and that at least it was his comfort that he understood his duty, though he did not understand these confounding Appearances. In this effort I succeeded far better than in the attempt to reason him out of his conviction. He became calm; the occupations incidental to his post as the night advanced began to make larger demands on his attention: and I left him at two in the morning. I had offered to stay through the night, but he would not hear of it.

That I more than once looked back at the red light as I ascended the pathway, that I did not like the red light, and that I should have slept but poorly if my bed had been under it, I see no reason to conceal. Nor did I like the two sequences of the accident and the dead girl. I see no reason to conceal that either.

But what ran most in my thoughts was the consideration how ought I to act, having become the recipient of this disclosure? I had proved the man to be intelligent, vigilant, painstaking, and exact; but how long might he remain so, in his state of mind? Though in a subordinate position, still he held a most important trust, and would I (for instance) like to stake my own life on the chances of his continuing to execute it with precision?

Unable to overcome a feeling that there would be something treacherous in my communicating what he had told me to his superiors in the company, without first being plain with himself and proposing a middle course to him, I ultimately resolved to offer to accompany him (otherwise keeping his secret for the present) to the wisest medical practitioner we could hear of in those parts, and to take his opinion. A change in his time of duty would come round next night, he had apprised me, and he would be off an hour or two after sunrise, and on again soon after sunset. I had appointed to return accordingly.

Next evening was a lovely evening, and I walked out early to enjoy it. The sun was not yet quite down when I traversed the field-path near the top of the deep cutting. I would extend my walk for an hour, I said to myself, half an hour on and half an hour back, and it would then be time to go to my signal-man's box.

Before pursuing my stroll, I stepped to the brink, and mechanically looked down, from the point from which I had first seen him. I cannot describe the thrill that seized upon me, when, close at the mouth of the tunnel, I saw the appearance of a man, with his left sleeve across his eyes, passionately waving his right arm.

The nameless horror that oppressed me passed in a moment, for in a moment I saw that this appearance of a man was a man indeed, and that there was a little group of other men, standing at a short distance, to whom he seemed to be rehearsing the gesture he made. The Danger-light was not yet lighted. Against its shaft, a little low hut, entirely new to me, had been made of some wooden supports and tarpaulin. It looked no bigger than a bed.

With an irresistible sense that something was wrong—with a flashing self-reproachful fear that fatal mischief had come of my leaving the man there, and causing no one to be sent to overlook or correct what he did—I descended the notched path with all the speed I could make.

"What is the matter?" I asked the men.

"Signal-man killed this morning, sir."

"Not the man belonging to that box?"

"Yes, sir."

"Not the man I know?"

"You will recognise him, sir, if you knew him," said the man who spoke for the others, solemnly uncovering his own head, and raising an end of the tarpaulin, "for his face is quite composed."

"O, how did this happen, how did this happen?" I asked, turning from one to another as the hut closed in again.

"He was cut down by an engine, sir. No man in England knew his work better. But somehow he was not clear of the outer rail. It was just at broad day. He had struck the light, and had the lamp in his hand. As the engine came out of the tunnel, his back was towards her, and she cut him down. That man drove her, and was showing how it happened. Show the gentleman, Tom."

The man, who wore a rough dark dress, stepped back to his former place at the mouth of the tunnel.

"Coming round the curve in the tunnel, sir," he said, "I saw him at the end, like as if I saw him down a perspective-glass. There was no time to check speed, and I knew him to be very careful. As he didn't seem to take heed of the whistle, I shut it off when we were running down upon him, and called to him as loud as I could call."

"What did you say?"

"I said, 'Below there! Look out! Look out! For God's sake, clear the way!'"

I started.

"Ah! it was a dreadful time, sir. I never left off calling to him. I put this arm before my eyes not to see, and I waved this arm to the last; but it was no use."

Without prolonging the narrative to dwell on any one of its curious circumstances more than on any other, I may, in closing it, point out the coincidence that the warning of the engine-driver included, not only the words which the unfortunate signal-man had repeated to me as haunting him, but also the words which I myself—not he—had attached, and that only in my own mind, to the gesticulation he had imitated.

Pumpkin-Decorating Good Times

Making jack-o-lanterns is a great Halloween tradition. A good way to decorate pumpkins for little ones is to paint directly on the pumpkins with poster paints. You can get small pumpkins and decorate a bunch of them. You can also get a pumpkin for each member of the family—differently shaped pumpkins for each person. Whether you carve the jack-o-lantern or paint it, here are some great designs you can use:

WOOOOOOO

The Sweeper

by A.M. Burrage

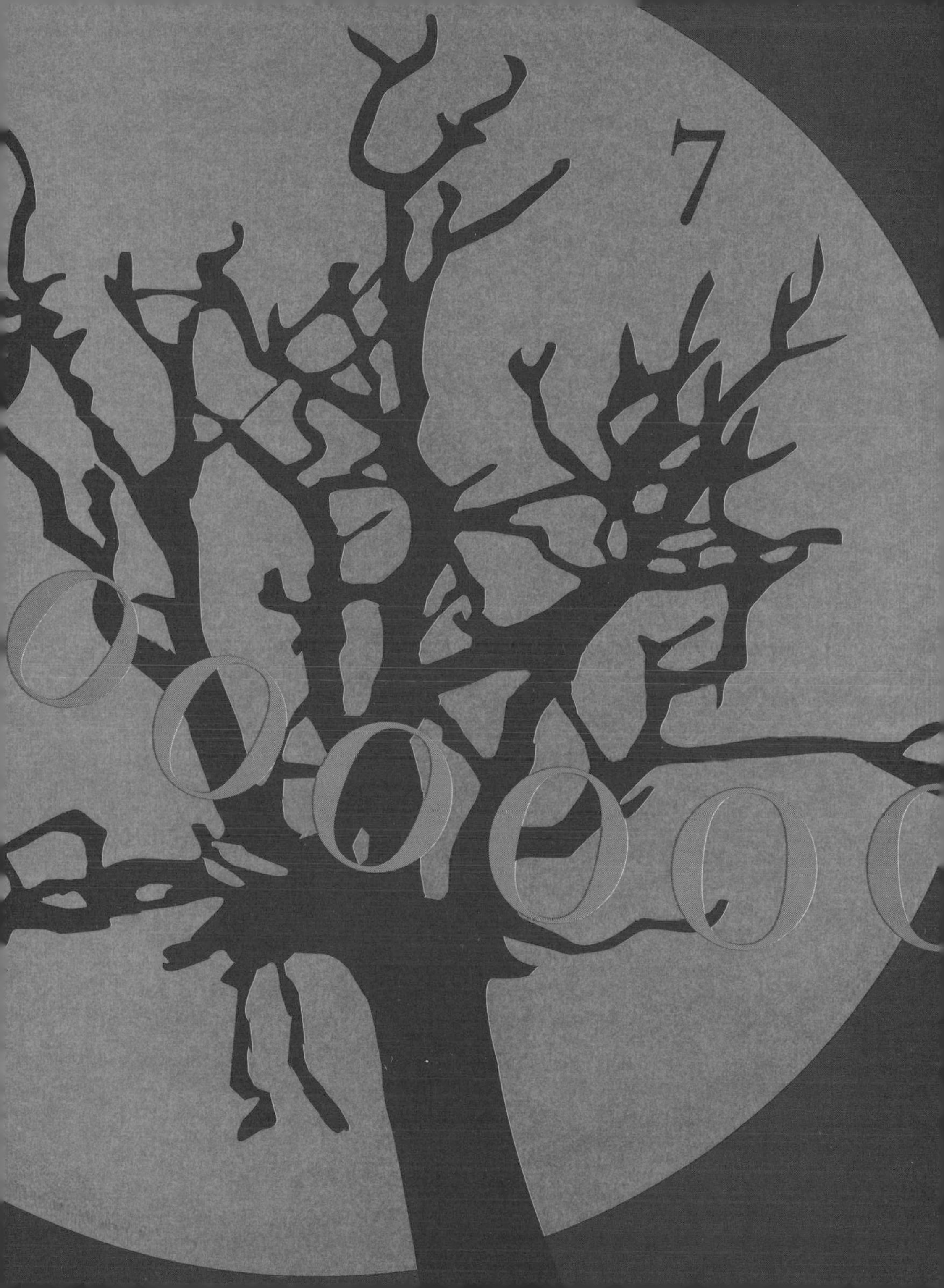
7

Woooooo

It seemed to Tessa Winyard that Miss Ludgate's strangest characteristic was her kindness to beggars. This was something more than a little peculiar in a nature which, to be sure, presented a surface like a mountain range of unexpected peaks and valleys; for there was a thin streak of meanness in her. One caught glimpses of it here and there, to be traced a little way and lost, like a thin elusive vein in a block of marble. One week she would pay the household bills without a murmur; the next she would simmer over them in a mild rage, questioning the smallest item, and suggesting the most absurd little economies which she would have been the first to condemn later if Mrs. Finch the housekeeper had ever taken her at her word. She was rich enough to be indifferent, but old enough to be crotchety.

Miss Ludgate gave very sparsely to local charities, and those good busybodies who went forth at different times with subscription lists and tales of good causes often visited her and came away empty. She had plausible, transparent excuses for keeping her purse-strings tight. Hospitals should be State-aided; schemes for assisting the poor destroyed thrift; we had heathens of our own to convert and needed to send no missionaries abroad. Yet she was sometimes overwhelmingly generous in her spasmodic charities to individuals, and her kindness to itinerant beggars was proverbial among their fraternity. Her neighbors were not grateful to her for this, for it was said that she encouraged every doubtful character who came that way.

When she first agreed to come on a month's trial, Tessa Winyard had known that she would find Miss Ludgate difficult, doubting whether she would be able to retain the post of companion, and, still more, if she would want to retain it. The thing was not arranged through the reading and answering of an advertisement. Tessa knew a married niece of the old lady who, while recommending the young girl to her ancient kinswoman, was able to give Tessa hints as to the nature and treatment of the old lady's crotchets. So she came to the house well instructed and not quite as a stranger.

Tessa came under the spell of the house from the moment when she entered it for the first time. She had an ingrained romantic love of old country mansions, and Billingdon Abbots, although nothing was left of the original priory after which it was named, was old enough to be worshipped. It was mainly Jacobean, but some eighteenth-century owner, a devotee of the then-fashionable cult of Italian architecture, had covered the façade with stucco and added a pillared portico. It was probably the same owner who had erected a summer-house to the design of a Greek temple at the end of a walk between nut bushes and who was responsible for the imitation ruin—to which Time had since added the authentic touch—beside the reedy fishpond at the rear of the house. Likely enough, thought Tessa, who knew the period, that same romantic squire was wont to engage an imitation "hermit" to meditate beside the spurious ruin on moonlight nights.

The gardens around the house were well wooded, and thus lent the house itself an air of melancholy and the inevitable slight atmosphere of damp and darkness. And here and there, in the most unexpected places, were garden gods, mostly broken and all in need of scouring. Tessa soon discovered these stone ghosts quite unexpectedly, and nearly always with a leap and tingle of surprise. A noseless Hermes confronted one at the turn of a shady walk; Demeter, minus a hand, stood half hidden by laurels, still keeping vigil for Persephone; a dancing faun stood poised and caught in a frozen caper by the gate of the walled-in kitchen garden; beside a small stone pond a satyr leered from his pedestal, as if waiting for a naiad to break the surface.

The interior of the house was at first a little awe-inspiring to Tessa. She loved pretty things, but she was inclined to be afraid of furniture and pictures which seemed to her to be coldly beautiful and conscious of their own intrinsic values. Everything was highly polished, spotless, and speckless, and the reception rooms had an air of state apartments thrown open for the inspection of the public.

The hall was square and galleried, and one could look straight up to the top storey and see the slanting balustrades of three staircases. Two suits of armour faced one across a parquet floor, and on the walls were three or four portraits by Lely and Kneller, those once fashionable painters of Court beauties whose works have lost favour with the collectors of today. The dining-room was long, rectangular, and severe, furnished only with a Cromwellian table and chairs and a great plain sideboard gleaming with silver candelabra. Two large seventeenth-century portraits by unknown members of the Dutch School were the only decorations bestowed on the panelled walls, and the window curtains were brown to match the one strip of carpet which the long table almost exactly covered.

Less monastic, but almost as severe and dignified, was the drawing-room in which Tessa spent most of her time with Miss Ludgate. The boudoir was a homelier room, containing such human things as photographs of living people, work-baskets, friendly armchairs, and a cosy, feminine atmosphere; but Miss Ludgate preferred more often to sit in state in her great drawing-room with the "Portrait of Miss Olivia Ludgate" by Gainsborough, the Chippendale furniture, and the cabinet of priceless china. It was as if she realized that she was but the guardian of her treasures and wanted to have them within sight now that her term of guardianship was drawing to a close.

She must have been well over eighty, Tessa thought; for she was very small and withered and frail, with that almost porcelain delicacy peculiar to certain very old ladies. Winter and summer, she wore a white woollen shawl inside the house, thick or thin according to the season, which matched in colour and to some extent texture her soft and still plentiful hair. Her face and hands were yellow-brown with the veneer of old age, but her hands were blue-veined, light and delicate, so that her fingers seemed overweighted by the simplest rings. Her eyes were blue and still piercing, and her mouth, once beautiful, was caught up at the corners by puckerings of the upper lip, and looked grim in repose. Her voice had not shrilled and always she spoke very slowly with an unaffected precision, as one who knew that she had only to be understood to be obeyed and therefore took care always to be understood.

Tessa spent her first week with Miss Ludgate without knowing whether or not she liked the old lady, or whether or not she was afraid of her. Nor was she any wiser with regard to Miss Ludgate's sentiments towards herself. Their relations were much as they might have been had Tessa been a child and Miss Ludgate a new governess suspected of severity. Tessa was on her best behaviour, doing as she was told and thinking before she spoke, as children should and generally do not. At times it occurred to her to wonder that Miss Ludgate had not sought to engage an older woman, for in the cold formality of that first week's intercourse she wondered what gap in the household she was supposed to fill, and what return she was making for her wage and board.

Truth to tell, Miss Ludgate wanted to see somebody young about the house, even if she could share with her companion no more than the common factors of their sex and their humanity. The servants were all old retainers kept faithful to her by rumours of legacies. Her relatives were few and immersed in their own affairs. The house and the bulk of the property from which she derived her income were held in trust for an heir appointed by the same will which had given her a life interest in the estate. It saved her from the transparent attentions of any fortune-hunting nephew or niece, but it kept her lonely and starved for young companionship.

It happened that Tessa was able to play the piano quite reasonably well and that she had an educated taste in music. So had Miss Ludgate, who had been a performer of much the same quality until the time came when her rebel fingers stiffened with rheumatism. So the heavy grand piano, which had been scrupulously kept in tune, was silent no longer, and Miss Ludgate regained an old lost pleasure. It should be added that Tessa was twenty-two and, with no pretensions to technical beauty, was rich in commonplace good looks which were enhanced by perfect health and the freshness of her youth. She looked her best in candlelight, with her slim hands—they at least would have pleased an artist—hovering like white moths over the keyboard of the piano.

When she had been with Miss Ludgate a week, the old lady addressed her for the first time as "Tessa." She added: "I hope you intend to stay with me, my dear. It will be dull for you, and I fear you will often find me a bother. But I shan't take up all your time, and I dare say you will be able to find friends and amusements."

So Tessa stayed on, and beyond the probationary month. She was a soft-hearted girl who gave her friendship easily but always sincerely. She tried to like everybody who liked her, and generally succeeded. It would be hard to analyse the quality of the friendship between the two women, but certainly it existed and at times they were able to touch hands over the barrier between youth and age. Miss Ludgate inspired in Tessa a queer tenderness. With all her wealth and despite her domineering manner, she was a pathetic and lonely figure. She reminded Tessa of some poor actress playing the part of Queen, wearing the tawdry crown jewels, uttering commands which the other mummers obeyed like automata; while all the while there awaited her the realities of life at the fall of the curtain—the wet streets, the poor meal, and the cold, comfortless lodging.

It filled Tessa with pity to think that here, close beside her, was a living, breathing creature, still clinging to life, who must, in the course of nature, so soon let go her hold. Tessa could think: "Fifty years hence I shall be seventy-two, and there's no reason why I shouldn't live till then." She wondered painfully how it must feel to be unable to look a month hence with average confidence, and to regard every nightfall as the threshold of a precarious tomorrow.

Tessa would have found life very dull but for the complete change in her surroundings. She had been brought up in a country vicarage, one of seven brothers and sisters who had worn one another's clothes, tramped the carpets threadbare, mishandled the cheap furniture, broken everything tangible except their parents' hearts, and had somehow tumbled into adolescence. The unwonted "grandeur" of living with Miss Ludgate flavoured the monotony.

We have her writing home to her "Darling Mother" as follows:

> I expect when I get back home again our dear old rooms will look absurdly small. I thought at first that the house was huge, and every room as big as a barrack-room—not that I've ever been in a barrack-room! But I'm getting used to it now, and really it isn't so enormous as I thought. Huge compared with ours, of course, but not so big as Lord Branbourne's house, or even Colonel Exted's.
>
> Really, though, it's a darling old place and might have come out of one of those books in which there's a Mystery, and a Sliding Panel, and the heroine's a nursery governess who marries the Young Baronet. But there's no mystery that I've heard of, although I like to pretend there is, and even if I were the nursery governess there's no young baronet within a radius of miles. But at least it ought to have a traditional ghost, although, since I haven't heard of one, it's probably deficient even in that respect! I don't like to ask Miss Ludgate, because, although she's a dear, there are questions I couldn't ask her. She might believe in ghosts and it might scare her to talk about them; or she mightn't, and then she'd be furious with me for talking rubbish. Of course, I know it's all rubbish, but it would be nice to know that we were supposed to be haunted by a nice Grey Lady—of, say, about the period of Queen Anne. But if we're haunted by nothing else, we're certainly haunted by tramps.

Her letter went on to describe the numerous daily visits of those nomads of the English countryside, who beg and steal on their way from workhouse to workhouse; those queer, illogical, feckless beings who prefer the most intense miseries and hardships to the comparative comforts attendant on honest work. Three or four was a day's average of such callers, and not one went away empty. Mrs. Finch had very definite orders, and she carried them out with the impassive face of a perfect subject of discipline. When there was no spare food, there was the pleasanter alternative of money which could be transformed into liquor at the nearest inn.

Tessa was forever meeting these vagrants in the drive. Male and female, they differed in a hundred ways; some still trying to cling to the last rags of self-respect, others obscene, leering, furtive, potential criminals who lacked the courage to rise above petty theft. Most faces were either evil or carried the rolling eyes and lewd, loose mouth of the semi-idiot, but they were all alike in their personal uncleanliness and in the insolence of their bearing.

Tessa grew used to receiving from them direct and insolent challenges of the eyes, familiar nods, blatant grins. In their several ways, they told her that she was nobody and that, if she hated to see them, so much the better. They knew she was an underling, subject to dismissal, whereas they, for some occult reason, were always the welcome guests. Tessa resented their presence and their dumb insolence, and secretly raged against Miss Ludgate for encouraging them. They were the sewer rats of society, foul, predatory, and carrying disease from village to village and from town to town.

The girl knew something of the struggles of the decent poor. Her upbringing in a country vicarage had given her intimate knowledge of farm-hands and builders' labourers, the tragic poverty of their homes, their independence and their gallant struggles for existence. On Miss Ludgate's estate, there was more than one family living on bread and potatoes and getting not too much of either. Yet the old lady had no sympathy for them, and gave unlimited largess to the undeserving. In the ditches outside the park, it was always possible to find a loaf or two of bread flung there by some vagrant who had feasted more delicately on the proceeds of a visit to the tradesmen's door.

It was not for Tessa to speak to Miss Ludgate on the subject. Indeed, she knew that—in the phraseology of the servants' hall—it was as much as her place was worth. But she did mention it to Mrs. Finch, whose duty was to provide food and drink, or failing those, money.

Mrs. Finch, taciturn through her environment but still with an undercurrent of warmth, replied at first with one pregnant word, "Orders!" After a moment she added: "The mistress has her own good reasons for doing it—or thinks she has."

It was late summer when Tessa first took up her abode at Billingdon Abbots, and sweet lavender, that first herald of the approach of autumn, was already blooming in the gardens. September came and the first warning gleams of yellow showed among the trees. Spiked chestnut husks opened and dropped their polished brown fruit. At evenings the ponds and the trout stream exhaled pale, low-hanging mists. There was a cold snap in the air.

By looking from her window every morning, Tessa marked on the trees the inexorable progress of the year. Day by day the green tints lessened as the yellow increased. Then yellow began to give place to gold and brown and red. Only the hollies and the laurels stood fast against the advancing tide.

There came an evening when Miss Ludgate appeared for the first time in her winter shawl. She seemed depressed and said little during dinner, and afterwards in the drawing room, when she had taken out and arranged a pack of patience cards preparatory to beginning her evening game, she suddenly leaned her elbows on the table and rested her face between her hands.

"Aren't you well, Miss Ludgate?" Tessa asked anxiously.

She removed her hands and showed her withered old face. Her eyes were piteous, fear-haunted, and full of shadows.

"I am very much as usual, my dear," she said. "You must bear with me. My bad time of year is just approaching. If I can live until the end of November I shall last another year. But I don't know yet—I don't know."

"Of course you're not going to die this year," said Tessa, with a robust note of optimism which she had found useful in soothing frightened children.

"If I don't die this autumn it will be the next, or some other autumn," quavered the old voice. "It will be in the autumn that I shall die. I know that. I know that."

"But how can you know?" Tessa asked, with just the right note of gentle incredulity.

"I know it. What does it matter how I know?...Have many leaves fallen yet?"

"Hardly any as yet," said Tessa. "There has been very little wind."

"They will fall presently," said Miss Ludgate. "Very soon now..."

Her voice trailed away, but presently she rallied, picked up the miniature playing cards, and began her game.

Two days later it rained heavily all the morning and throughout the earlier part of the afternoon. Just as the light was beginning to wan, half a gale of wind sprang up, and showers of yellow leaves, circling and eddying at the wind's will, began to find their way to earth through the level slant of the rain. Miss Ludgate sat watching them, her eyes dull with the suffering of despair, until the lights were turned on and the blinds were drawn.

During dinner the wind dropped again and the rain ceased. Tessa afterwards peeped between the blinds to still silhouettes of trees against the sky, and a few stars sparkling palely. It promised after all to be a fine night.

As before, Miss Ludgate got out her patience cards, and Tessa picked up a book and waited to be bidden to go to the piano. There was silence in the room save for intermittent sounds of cards being laid with a snap upon the polished surface of the table, and occasional dry rustlings as Tessa turned the pages of her book.

...When she first heard it Tessa could not truthfully have said. It seemed to her that she had gradually become conscious of the sounds in the garden outside, and when at last they had forced themselves upon her attention as to set her wondering what caused them, it was impossible for her to guess how long they had actually been going on.

Tessa closed the book over her fingers and listened. The sounds were crisp, dry, long-drawn-out, and rhythmic. There was an equal pause after each one. It was rather like listening to the leisurely brushing of a woman's long hair. What was it? An uneven surface being scratched by something crisp and pliant? Then Tessa knew. On the long path behind the house which travelled the whole length of the building somebody was sweeping up the fallen leaves with a stable broom. But what a time to sweep up leaves!

She continued to listen. Now that she had identified the sounds they were quite unmistakable. She would not have had to guess twice had it not been dark outside, and the thought of a gardener showing such devotion to duty as to work at that hour had at first been rejected by her subconscious mind. She looked up, with the intention of making some remark to Miss Ludgate—and she said nothing.

Miss Ludgate sat listening intently, her face half turned towards the windows and slightly raised, her eyes upturned. Her whole attitude was one of strained rigidity, expressive of a tension rather dreadful to see in one so old. Tessa not only listened, she now watched.

There was a movement in the unnaturally silent room. Miss Ludgate had turned her head and now showed her companion a white face of woe and doom-ridden eyes. Then, in a flash, her expression changed. Tessa knew that Miss Ludgate had caught her listening to the sounds from the path outside, and that for some reason the old lady was annoyed with her for having heard them. But why? And why that look of terror on the poor, white, old face?

"Won't you play something, Tessa?"

Despite the note of interrogation, the words were an abrupt command, and Tessa knew it. She was to drown the noise of sweeping from outside, because for some queer reason, Miss Ludgate did not want her to hear it. So, tactfully, she played pieces which allowed her to make liberal use of the loud pedal.

After half an hour Miss Ludgate rose, gathered her shawl tighter about her shoulders, and hobbled to the door, pausing on the way to say good night to Tessa.

Tessa lingered in the room alone and reseated herself before the piano. A minute or two elapsed before she began to strum softly and absent-mindedly. Why did Miss Ludgate object to her hearing that sound of sweeping from the path outside? It had ceased now, or she would have peeped out to see who actually was at work.

Had Miss Ludgate some queer distaste for seeing fallen leaves lying about, and was she ashamed because she was keeping a gardener at work at that hour? But it was unlike Miss Ludgate to mind what people thought of her; besides, she rose late in the morning, and there would be plenty of time to brush away the leaves before the mistress of the house could set eyes on them. And then, why was Miss Ludgate so terrified? Had it anything to do with her queer belief that she would die in the autumn?

On her way to bed Tessa smiled gently to herself for having tried to penetrate to the secret places of a warped mind which was over eighty years old. She had just seen another queer phase of Miss Ludgate, and all of such seemed inexplicable.

The night was calm and promised so to remain.

"There won't be many more leaves down tonight," Tessa reflected as she undressed.

But when next morning she sauntered out into the garden before breakfast, the long path which skirted the rear of the house was still thickly littered with them, and Toy, the second gardener, was busy among them with a barrow and one of those birch stable brooms which, in mediaeval imaginations, provided steeds for witches.

"Hullo!" exclaimed Tessa. "What a lot of leaves must have come down last night!"

Toy ceased sweeping and shook his head.

"No, miss. This 'ere little lot came down with the wind early part o' the evening."

"But surely they were all swept up. I heard somebody at work here after nine o'clock. Wasn't that you?"

The man grinned.

"You catch any of us at work after nine o'clock, miss!" he said. "No, miss, nobody's touched 'em till now. 'Tis thankless work, too.

So soon as you've swept up one lot there's another waitin'. Not a hundred men could keep this 'ere garden tidy this time o' the year."

Tessa said nothing more and went thoughtfully into the house. The sweeping was continued off and on all day, for more leaves descended, and a bonfire built up on the waste ground beyond the kitchen garden wafted its fragrance over to the house.

That evening Miss Ludgate had a fire made up in the boudoir and announced to Tessa that they would sit there before and after dinner. But it happened that the chimney smoked, and after coughing and grumbling and rating Mrs. Finch on the dilatoriness and inefficiency of sweeps, the old lady went early to bed.

It was still too early for Tessa to retire. Having been left to herself, she remember a book which she had left in the drawing room, and with which she purposed sitting over the dining-room fire. Hardly had she taken two steps past the threshold of the drawing room when she came abruptly to a halt and stood listening. She could not doubt the evidence of her ears. In spite of what Toy had told her, and that it was now after half past nine, somebody was sweeping the path outside.

She tiptoed to the window and peeped out between the blinds. Bright moonlight silvered the garden, but she could see nothing. Now, however, that she was near the window, she could locate the sounds more accurately, and they seemed to proceed from a spot farther down the path which was hidden from her by the angle of the window setting. There was a door just outside the room giving access to the garden, but for no reason that she could name, she felt strangely unwilling to go out and look at the mysterious worker. With the strangest little cold thrill she was aware of a distinct preference for seeing him—for the first time, at least—from a distance.

Then Tessa remembered a landing window, and after a little hesitation she went silently and on tiptoe upstairs to the first floor and down a passage on the left of the stairhead. Here moonlight penetrated a window and threw a pale blue screen upon the opposite wall. Tessa fumbled with the window fastening, raised the sash softly and silently, and leaned out.

On the path below her, but some yards to her left and close to the angle of the house, a man was slowly and rhythmically sweeping with a stable broom. The broom swung struck the path time after time with a soft, crisp *swish*, and the strokes were as regular as those of the pendulum of some slow old clock.

From her angle of observation, she was unable to see most of the characteristics of the figure underneath. It was that of a working-man, for there was something in the silhouette subtly suggestive of old and baggy clothes. But apart from all else there was something queer, something odd and unnatural, in the scene on which she gazed. She knew that there was somcthing lacking, something that she should have found missing at the first glance, yet for her life she could not have said what it was.

From below some gross omission blazed past her, and though she was acutely aware that the scene lacked something which she had every right to expect to see, her senses groped for it in vain; although the lack of something which should have been there, and was not, was as obvious as a burning pyre at midnight. She knew that she was watching the gross defiance of some natural law; she withdrew her head.

All the cowardice in Tessa's nature urged her to go to bed, to forget what she had seen, and to refrain from trying to remember what she had *not* seen. But the other Tessa, the Tessa who despised cowards, and was herself capable under pressure of rising to great heights of courage, stayed and urged. Under her rising breath, she talked to herself, as she always did when any crisis found her in a state of indecision.

"Tessa, you coward! How dare you be afraid! Go down at once and see who it is and what's queer about him. He can't eat you!"

So the two Tessas imprisoned in one body stole downstairs again, and the braver Tessa was angry with their common heart for thumping so hard and trying to weaken her. But she unfastened the door and stepped out into the moonlight.

The Sweeper was still at work close to the angle of the house, near by where the path ended and a green door gave entrance to the stable yard. The path was thick with leaves, and the girl, advancing uncertainly with her hands to her breasts, saw that he was making little progress with his work. The broom rose and fell and audibly swept the path, but the dead leaves lay fast and still beneath it. Yet it was not this that she had noticed from above. There was still that unseizable Something missing.

Her footfalls made little noise on the leaf-strewn path, but they became audible to the Sweeper while she was still half a dozen yards from him. He paused in his work and turned and looked at her.

He was a tall, lean man with a white cadaverous face and eyes that bulged like huge rising bubbles as they regarded her. It was a foul, suffering face which he showed to Tessa, a face whose misery could—and did—inspire loathing and a hitherto unimagined horror, but never pity. He was clad in the meanest rags, which seemed to have been cast at random over his emaciated body. The hands grasping the broom seemed no more than bones and skin. He was so thin, thought Tessa, that he was almost—and here she paused in thought, because she found herself hating the word which tried to force itself into her mind. But it had its way and blew in on a cold wind of terror. Yes, he was almost transparent, she thought, and sickened at the word, which had come to have a new and vile meaning for her.

They faced each other through a fraction of eternity not to be measured by seconds; and then Tessa heard herself scream. It flashed upon her now, the strange, abominable detail of the figure which confronted her—the Something missing which she had noticed, without actually seeing, from above. The path was flooded with moonlight, but the visitant had no shadow. And fast upon this vile discovery she saw dimly *through* it the ivy stirring upon the wall. Then, as unbidden thoughts rushed to tell her that the Thing was not of the world and that it was not holy, and the sudden knowledge wrung that scream from her, so she was left suddenly and dreadfully alone. The spot where the Thing had stood was empty save for the moonlight and the shallow litter of leaves.

Tessa had no memory of returning to the house. Her next recollection was of finding herself in the hall, faint and gasping and sobbing. Even as she approached the stairs she saw a light dancing on the wall above and wondered what fresh horror was to confront her. But it was only Mrs. Finch coming downstairs in a dressing gown, candle in hand, an incongruous but a very comforting sight.

"Oh, it's you, Miss Tessa," said Mrs. Finch, reassured. She held the candle lower and peered down at the sobbing girl. "Why, whatever is the matter? Oh, Miss Tessa, Miss Tessa! You haven't never been outside, have you?"

Tessa sobbed and choked and tried to speak.

"I've seen—I've seen…"

Mrs. Finch swiftly descended the remaining stairs and put an arm around the shuddering girl.

"Hush, my dear, my dear! I know what you've seen. You didn't ought never to have gone out. I've seen it too, once—but only once, thank God."

"What is it?" Tessa faltered.

"Never you mind, my dear. Now don't be frightened. It's all over now. He doesn't come here for you. It's the mistress he wants. You've nothing to fear, Miss Tessa. Where was he when you saw him?"

"Close to the end of the path, near the stable gate."

Mrs. Finch threw up her hands.

"Oh, the poor mistress—the poor mistress! Her time's shortening! The end's nigh now!"

"I can't bear anymore," Tessa sobbed; and then she contradicted herself, clinging to Mrs. Finch. "I must know. I can't rest until I know. Tell me everything."

"Come into my parlour, my dear, and I'll make you a cup of tea. We can both do with it, I think. But you'd best not know. At least not tonight, Miss Tessa—not tonight."

"I must," whispered Tessa, "if I'm ever to have any peace."

The fire was still burning behind a guard in the housekeeper's parlour, for Mrs. Finch had only gone up to bed a few minutes since. There was water still warm in the brass kettle, and in a few minutes the tea was ready. Tessa sipped and felt the first vibrations of her returning courage, and presently looked inquiringly at Mrs. Finch.

"I'll tell you, Miss Tessa," said the old housekeeper, "if it'll make you any easier. But don't let the mistress know as I've told you."

Tessa inclined her head and gave the required promise.

"You don't know why," Mrs. Finch began in a low voice, "the mistress gives to every beggar, deserving or otherwise. The reason come into what I'm going to tell you. Miss Ludgate wasn't always like that—not until up to about fifteen years ago.

"She was old then, but active for her age, and very fond of gardening. Late one afternoon in the autumn, while she was cutting some late roses, a beggar came to the tradesmen's door. Sick and ill and starved, he looked—but there, you've seen him. He was a bad lot, we found out afterwards, but I was sorry for him, and I was just going to risk givin' him some food without orders, when up comes Miss Ludgate. 'What's this?' she says.

"He whined something about not being able to get work.

"'Work!' says the mistress. 'You don't want work—you want charity. If you want to eat,' she says. 'you shall, but you shall work first. There's a broom,' she says, 'and there's a path littered with leaves. Start sweeping up at the top, and when you come to the end you can come and see me.'

"Well, he took the broom, and a few minutes later I heard a shout from Miss Ludgate and come hurryin' out. There was the man lyin' at the top of the path where he'd commenced sweeping, and he'd collapsed and fallen down. I didn't know then as he was dying, but he did, and he gave Miss Ludgate a look as I shall never forget.

"'When I've swept to the end of the path,' he says, 'I'll come for you, my lady, and we'll feast together. Only see as you're ready to be fetched when I come.' Those were his last words. He was buried by the parish, and it gave Miss Ludgate such a turn that she ordered something to be given to every beggar who came, and not one of 'em to be asked to do a stroke of work.

"But next autumn, when the leaves began to fall, he came back and started sweeping, right at the top of the path, round about where he died. We've all heard him and most of us have seen him. Year after year he's come back and swept with his broom, which just makes a brushing noise and hardly stirs a leaf. But each year he's been getting nearer and nearer to the end of the path, and when he gets right to the end—well, I wouldn't like to be the mistress, with all her money."

It was three evenings later, just before the hour fixed for dinner, that the Sweeper completed his task. That is to say, if one reposes literal belief in Mrs. Finch's story.

The servants heard somebody burst open the tradesmen's door, and, having rushed out into the passage, two of them saw that the door was open but found no one there. Miss Ludgate was already in the drawing room, but Tessa was still upstairs, dressing for dinner. Presently Mrs. Finch had occasion to enter the drawing room to speak to her mistress; and her screams warned the household of what had happened. Tessa heard them just as she was ready to go downstairs, and she rushed into the drawing room a few moments later.

Miss Ludgate was sitting upright in her favourite chair. Her eyes were open, but she was quite dead; and in her eyes there was something that Tessa could not bear to see.

Withdrawing her own gaze from that fixed stare of terror and recognition, she saw something on the carpet and presently stooped to pick it up.

It was a little yellow leaf, damp and pinched and frayed, and but for her own experience and Mrs. Finch's tale she might have wondered how it had come to be there. She dropped it, shuddering, for it looked as if it has been picked up by, and had afterwards fallen from, the birch twigs of a stable broom.

Horrifying Halloween Game #1

Worm Pie

You will need several pie tins (shallow bowls, or large plates will also work) for this game—one per player. Fill each pie tin up with an equal number of gummy worms (20–25) and then cover the worms generously with whipped cream or Cool Whip. Using an egg timer, give the kids a three-minute time limit, or better yet, use a good Halloween song, like "The Monster Mash," to start and end the game. Each player must pull out as many worms as possible using only his or her mouth in the time allotted. When the time's up (or the music stops) the child with the most worms wins. The more mess you make, the more fun you—and the people watching—will have!

8

The Baby-Sitter

a folk tale

chop
chop
chop

chop

chop

ollie was baby-sitting for the Gustafsons on a Saturday night in October. It was nine o'clock, and the children, a five-year-old girl named Amy and a three-year-old boy named Peter, were upstairs sleeping. The Gustafsons were at a Halloween party and probably wouldn't be home till well after midnight.

Mollie was watching a movie on the couch and snacking on some popcorn when the phone rang. She thought it might be the Gustafsons calling to check in, but on the other end of the line was silence.

"Hello?" she said.

A man's voice came on the line, throaty and deep, "Have you checked on the children?" he asked.

"Who is this?" she said. It did not sound like Mr. Gustafson.

"I'm coming at 10:30, and I'm going to kill the children, and then I'm going to kill you."

Mollie slammed the phone down, angry and upset. The call had disturbed her, but she figured it was only a stupid prank. Still, to make herself feel better, she went upstairs to check on the kids.

Peter and Amy were fast asleep in their beds, and all was quiet. *What a jerk!* she thought, and she came back downstairs to resume her movie. Soon, she forgot all about the prank call.

At 9:30, the phone rang again. Mollie picked up the receiver. "Hello?" she said.

"Have you checked on the children?" the man's voice asked. "Because at 10:30, I'm going to kill the children, and then I'm going to kill you."

Mollie slammed the phone down again, more annoyed than frightened this time. *Whoever's making those calls has a really sick sense of humor*, she thought. She guessed it was probably one of the boys from school, who would get a big kick out of that sort of thing.

The third time the man called, it was ten o'clock. "Only a half-hour left before I come for the children and then you," he said. This time, Mollie decided to call the police. That would teach the prank caller. She called the police and told the dispatcher what was going on. "All right," the dispatcher said. "If he calls back again, try to keep him on the line, and we'll put a tracer on the call."

After almost half an hour, the phone rang again, and Mollie ran to answer it. She tried to talk to the man to keep him on longer, but all he said was, "It won't be long now before I kill the children, and then come to kill you."

Mollie was getting more worried. *Why would anybody want to scare me like this?* she thought. *What if someone really did try to break into the house?* A few minutes later, she heard the phone ring. "Who is this?" she blurted out.

"It's the police, miss. You need to get out of there immediately. We've traced the call, and it's coming from inside the house. Get outside just as fast as you can and wait for the police. We're sending two squad cars over, and they should be there in a few minutes."

Mollie, petrified, dropped the phone and ran toward the front door. But before she could get make it to the door, she froze as she saw a stocky, middle-aged man in a blue flannel shirt, blocking the way out. He was holding an axe in his right hand, and there was blood splattered all over his arms, legs, and black boots—and a trail of blood leading all the way up the stairs. It was the man who had been calling her all night. He had been making the calls from the upstairs phone. He had been in the house the whole time.

She screamed and screamed for help as he grabbed her, held her down, and lifted the axe over his shoulder. He struck her with the blade and then brought the axe down on her again and again. The police were too late. When they got to the house several minutes later, they found all that was left of Mollie inside the front door, and the bodies of Peter and Amy upstairs in their blood-soaked beds.

chop.

Horrifying Halloween Game #2

Dead Man's Brains

Gather everyone in a circle, turn down the lights, and tell them the story of the baby-sitter and the axe murderer. Tell them that when the police finally caught up with the madman, they were forced to shoot and kill him. That was years ago. But tonight, you have his remains. Pass around for everyone to feel:

his brains (a large, wet, squishy tomato or a large bunch of cooked cauliflower)

his eyes (two peeled grapes)

his nose (an appropriately sized chicken bone)

his ear (a fig or dried apricot)

his hand (a cloth glove filled with cold mud)

his heart (a piece of raw liver or a peeled tomato)

his blood (a bowl of ketchup thinned with warm water or corn syrup dyed red and thinned with warm water)

and his guts (a handful of thick spaghetti or linguini, cooked and wet).

9

Mister Ice Cold

dingy, di-ding

by Gahan Wilson

hear...

dingy, di-ding, dingy, di-ding

track 4

Listen, children! Hear the music? Hear its bright and cheerful chiming coming down the street? Hear it playing its pretty little tune—*dingy di-ding, dingy di-ding*—as it sings softly through the green trees, through the blue sky overhead, as it sings through the thick, still, sultry summer heat?

It's Mister Ice Cold coming in his truck! Mister Ice Cold and his nice ice cream! Fat, round, cool balls of it plopped into cones! Thick, juicy slabs of it covered in frozen chocolate frosting and stuck on sticks! Soft, pink, chilly twirls of it oozed into cups!

The music's coming closer through the heat—*dingy di-ding, dingy di-ding*—and excitement starts stirring where all was lazy and drowsy just a sweaty blink before!

Bobby Martin's no longer lying flat on the grass, staring up at a slow-moving summer cloud without seeing it at all; he's scrambled to his feet and is running over the thick summer grass to ask his mother—nodding on the porch over a limp magazine almost slipped from her fingers—if he can have enough money to buy a frozen lime frog.

And Suzy Brenner's left off dreamily trying to tie her doll's bonnet over her cat's head (much to the cat's relief) and is desperately digging into her plastic, polka-dot purse to see if there's enough change in there to buy her a cup of banana ice cream with chocolate sprinkles. Oh, she can taste the sweetness of it! Oh, her throat can feel its coolness going down!

And you, you've forgotten all about blowing through a leaf to see if you can make it squeak the way you saw Arnold Carter's older brother do it; now you're clawing feverishly with your small hands in both pockets, feeling your way past that sandy shell you found yesterday on the beach, and that little ball chewed bounceless by your dog, and that funny rock you came across in the vacant lot which may, with luck, be full of uranium and highly radioactive, and so far you have come up with two pennies and a quarter and you think you've just touched a nickel.

Meantime Mister Ice Cold's truck is rolling ever closer—*dingy di-ding, dingy di-ding*—and Martin Walpole, always a showoff, wipes his brow, points, and calls out proudly: "I see it! There it is!"

And sure enough, *there it is,* rolling smoothly around the corner of Main and Lincoln, and you can see the shiny, fat fullness of its white roof gleaming in the bright sun through the thick, juicy-green foliage of the trees which have, in the peak of their summer swelling, achieved a tropical density and richness more appropriate to some Amazonian jungle than to midwestern Lakeside, and you push aside one last, forgotten tangle of knotted string in your pocket and your heart swells for joy because you've come across another quarter and that means you've got enough for an orange icicle on a stick which will freeze your fillings and chill your gut and stain your tongue that gorgeous, glowing copper color which never fails to terrify your sister!

Now Mister Ice Cold's truck has swept into full view and its *dingy di-ding* sounds out loud and clear and sprightly enough, even in this steaming, muggy air, to startle a sparrow and make it swerve in its flight.

Rusty Taylor's dog barks for a signal, and all of you come running quick as you can from every direction, coins clutched in your sweaty fingers and squeezed tightly as possible in your damp, small palms, and every one of you is licking your lips and staring at the bright-blue lettering painted in frozen ice cubes and spelling out MISTER ICE COLD over the truck's sides and front and back, and Mister Ice Cold himself gives a sweeping wave of his big, pale hand to everyone from behind his wheel and brings his vehicle and all the wonders it contains to a slow, majestic halt with the skill and style of a commodore docking an ocean liner.

"A strawberry rocket!" cries fat Harold Smith, who has got there way ahead of everyone as usual, and Mister Ice Cold flips open one of the six small doors set into the left side of the truck with a *click* and plucks out Harold's rocket and gives it to him and takes the money, and before you know it he has smoothly glided to the right top door of the four doors at the truck's back and opened it, *click*, and Mandy Carter's holding her frozen maple tree and licking it and handing her money over all at the same time, and now Mister Ice Cold is opening one of the six small doors on the right side of the truck, *click*, and Eddy Morse has bitten the point off the top of his bright red cinnamon crunchy munch and is completely happy.

Then your heart's desire is plucked with a neat *click* from the top middle drawer on the truck's right side, which has always been its place for as long as you can remember, and you've put your money into Mister Ice Cold's large, pale, always cool palm, and as you step back to lick your orange icicle and to feel its coolness trickle down your throat, once again you find yourself admiring the sheer athletic smoothness of Mister Ice Cold's movements as he glides and dips, spins and turns, bows and rises, going from one small door, *click*, to another, *click*, with never a stumble, *click*, never a pause, *click*, his huge body leaving a coolness in the wake of his passing, and you wish you moved that smoothly when you ran back over the gravel of the playground with your hands stretched up, hoping for a catch, but you know you don't.

Everything's so familiar and comforting: the slow quieting of the other children getting what they want, your tongue growing ever more chilled as you reduce yet another orange icicle, lick by lick, down to its flat stick, and the heavy, hot summer air pressing down on top of it all.

But this time it's just a little different than it ever was before because, without meaning to, without having the slightest intention of doing it, you've noticed something you never noticed before. Mister Ice Cold never opens the bottom right door in the back of the truck.

He opens all the rest of them, absolutely every one, and you see him doing it now as new children arrive and call out what they want. *Click, click, click,* he opens them one after the other, producing frozen banana bars and cherry twirls and all the other special favorites, each one always from its particular, predictable door.

But his big, cool hand always glides past that *one door* set into the truck's back, the one on the bottom row, the one to the far right. And you realize now, with a funny little thrill, that you have never—not in all the years since your big brother Fred first took you by the hand and gave Mister Ice Cold the money for your orange icicle because you were so small you couldn't even count—you have never *ever* seen that door open.

And now you've licked the whole orange icicle away, and your tongue's moving over and over the rough wood of the stick without feeling it at all, and you can't stop staring at that door, and you know, deep in the pit of your stomach, that you have to open it.

You watch Mister Ice Cold carefully now, counting out to yourself how long it takes him to move from the doors farthest forward back to the rear of the truck, and because your mind is racing very, very quickly, you soon see that two orders in a row will keep him up front just long enough for you to open the door which is never opened, the door which you are now standing close enough to touch, just enough time to take a quick peek and close it shut before he knows.

Then Betty Deane calls out for a snow maiden right on top of Mike Howard's asking for a pecan pot, and you know those are both far up on the right-hand side.

Mister Ice Cold glides by you close enough for the cool breeze coming from his passing to raise little goose bumps on your arms. Without pausing, without giving yourself a chance for any more thought, you reach out.

Click!

Your heart freezes hard as anything inside the truck. There, inside the square opening, cold and bleached and glistening, are two tidy stacks of small hands, small as yours, their fingertips reaching out toward you and the sunlight, their thin, dead young arms reaching out behind them, back into the darkness. Poking over the top two hands, growing out of something shiny and far back and horribly still, are two stiff golden braids of hair with pretty frozen bows tied onto their ends.

But you have stared too long in horror and the door is closed, *click*, and almost entirely covered by Mister Ice Cold's hand, which now seems enormous, and he's bent down over you with his huge, smiling face so near to yours you can feel the coolness of it in the summer heat.

"Not that door," he says, very softly, and his small, neat, even teeth shine like chips from an iceberg, and because of his closeness now you know that even his breath is icy cold. "Those in there are not for you. Those in there are for me."

Then he's standing up again and moving smoothly from door to door, *click, click, click,* and none of the other children saw inside, and none of them will really believe you when you tell them, though their eyes will go wide and they'll love the story, and not a one of them saw the promise for you in Mister Ice Cold's eyes.

But you did, didn't you? And some night, after the end of summer, when it's cool and you don't want it any cooler, you'll be lying in your bed all alone and you'll hear Mister Ice Cold's pretty little song coming closer and closer through the night, through the dead, withered autumn leaves.

Dingy di-ding, dingy di-ding...

Then, later on, you just may hear the first *click*.

But you'll never hear the second *click*.

None of them ever do.

Horribly Good Halloween Goodies

Deviled Eyeballs

You will need:
one dozen eggs
two dozen green olives stuffed with pimientos
1 cup mayonnaise or Miracle Whip
2 tablespoons mustard

1. Hard boil the eggs. Let them cool and peel them.
2. Cut eggs in half lengthwise and remove the yolks.
3. Mix yolks, mayonnaise, and mustard until smooth, and spoon this mixture back into the egg halves.
4. Add one stuffed olive to the center of each egg, so that the pimiento is facing out, like a red pupil. Now you've got twenty-four delicious eyeballs!

Ghost Cake

Bake a cake in a rectangular cake pan (it can be from scratch or from any ready-to-make cake mix). To make the cake a "ghost cake," simply round off with a knife the top corners of the cake. Then frost the whole thing with white frosting. Add black jelly beans for the eyes and a licorice whip for the mouth. For an extra spooky touch, make red velvet cake, so that when you cut into your ghost cake, it will "bleed" red!

10

Harry

by Rosemary Timperley

shrieeeeeek

shrieeeeeek

shrieeeeeek
shrieeeeeek

Such ordinary things make me afraid. Sunshine. Sharp shadows on grass. White roses. Children with red hair. And the name—Harry. Such an ordinary name.

Yet the first time Christine mentioned the name, I felt a premonition of fear.

She was five years old, due to start school in three months' time. It was a hot, beautiful day, and she was playing alone in the garden, as she often did. I saw her lying on her stomach in the grass, picking daisies and making daisy-chains with laborious pleasure. The sun burned on her pale red hair and made her skin look very white. Her big blue eyes were wide with concentration.

Suddenly she looked towards the bush of white roses, which cast its shadow over the grass, and smiled.

"Yes, I'm Christine," she said. She rose and walked slowly towards the bush, her little plump legs defenceless and endearing beneath the too-short blue cotton skirt. She was growing fast.

"With my mummy and daddy," she said clearly. Then, after a pause, "Oh, but they *are* my mummy and daddy."

She was in the shadow of the bush now. It was as if she'd

walked out of the world of light into darkness. Uneasy, without quite knowing why, I called to her:

"Chris, what are you doing?"

"Nothing." The voice sounded too far away.

"Come indoors now. It's too hot for you out there."

"Not too hot."

"Come indoors, Chris."

She said: "I must go in now. Goodbye," then walked slowly towards the house.

"Chris, who were you talking to?"

"Harry," she said.

"Who's Harry?"

"Harry."

I couldn't get anything else out of her, so I just gave her some cake and milk and read to her until bedtime. As she listened, she stared out at the garden. Once she smiled and waved. It was a relief finally to tuck her up in bed and feel she was safe.

When Jim, my husband, came home I told him about the mysterious "Harry." He laughed.

"Oh, she's started that lark, has she?"

"What do you mean, Jim?"

"It's not so very rare for only children to have an imaginary companion. Some kids talk to their dolls. Chris has never been keen on her dolls. She hasn't any brothers or sisters. She hasn't any friends her own age. So she imagines someone."

"But why has she picked that particular name?"

He shrugged. "You know how kids pick things up. I don't know what you're worrying about, honestly I don't."

"Nor do I really. It's just that I feel extra responsible for her. More so than if I were her real mother."

"I know, but she's all right. Chris is fine. She's a pretty, healthy, intelligent little girl. A credit to you."

"And to you."

"In fact, we're thoroughly nice parents!"

"And so modest!"

We laughed together and he kissed me. I felt consoled.

Until the next morning.

Again the sun shone brilliantly on the small, bright lawn and white roses. Christine was sitting on the grass, cross-legged, staring towards the rose bush, smiling.

"Hello," she said. "I hoped you'd come...Because I like you. How old are you?...I'm only five and a piece...I'm *not* a baby! I'm going to school soon and I shall have a new dress. A green one. Do you go to school?...What do you do then?" She was silent for a while, nodding, listening, absorbed.

I felt myself going cold as I stood there in the kitchen. "Don't be silly. Lots of children have an imaginary companion," I told myself desperately. "Just carry on as if nothing were happening. Don't listen. Don't be a fool."

But I called Chris in earlier than usual for her midmorning milk.

"Your milk's ready, Chris. Come along."

"In a minute." This was a strange reply. Usually she rushed in eagerly for her milk and the special sandwich cream biscuits, over which she was a little gourmande.

"Come now, darling," I said.

"Can Harry come too?"

"No!" The cry burst from me harshly, surprising me.

"Goodbye, Harry. I'm sorry you can't come in, but I've got to have my milk," Chris said, then ran towards the house.

"Why can't Harry have some milk too?" she challenged me.

"Who *is* Harry, darling?"

"Harry's my brother."

"But, Chris, you haven't got a brother. Daddy and mummy have only got one child, one little girl, and that's you. Harry can't be your brother."

"Harry's my brother. He says so." She bent over the glass of milk and emerged with a smeary top lip. Then she grabbed at the biscuits. At least "Harry" hadn't spoilt her appetite!

After she'd had her milk, I said, "We'll go shopping now, Chris. You'd like to come to the shops with me, wouldn't you?"

"I want to stay with Harry."

"Well you can't. You're coming with me."

"Can Harry come too?"

"No."

My hands were trembling as I put on my hat and gloves. It was chilly in the house nowadays, as if there were a cold shadow over it in spite of the sun outside. Chris came with me meekly enough, but as we walked down the street, she turned and waved.

I didn't mention any of this to Jim that night. I knew he'd only scoff as he'd done before. But when Christine's "Harry" fantasy went on day after day, it got more and more on my nerves. I came to hate and dread those long summer days. I longed for gray skies and rain. I longed for the white roses to wither and die. I trembled when I heard Christine's voice prattling away in the garden. She talked quite unrestrainedly to "Harry" now.

One Sunday, when Jim heard her at it, he said: "I'll say one thing for imaginary companions, they help a child on with her talking. Chris is talking much more freely than she used to."

"With an accent," I blurted out.

"An accent?"

"A slight cockney accent."

"My dearest, every London child gets a slight cockney accent. It'll be much worse when she goes to school and meets lots of other kids."

"We don't talk cockney. Where does she get it from? Who can she be getting it from except Ha…" I couldn't say the name.

"The baker, the milkman, the dustman, the coalman, the window cleaner—want any more?"

"I suppose not." I laughed ruefully. Jim made me feel foolish.

"Anyway," said Jim, "*I* haven't noticed any cockney in her voice."

"There isn't when she talks to us. It's only when she's talking to—to him."

"To Harry. You know, I'm getting quite attached to young Harry. Wouldn't it be fun if one day we looked out and saw him?"

"Don't!" I cried. "Don't say that! It's my nightmare. My waking nightmare. Oh, Jim, I can't bear it much longer."

He looked astonished. "This Harry business is really getting you down, isn't it?"

"Of course it is! Day in, day out, I hear nothing but 'Harry this,' 'Harry that,' 'Harry says,' 'Harry thinks,' 'Can Harry have some?', 'Can Harry come too?'—it's all right for you out at the office all day, but I have to live with it: I'm—I'm afraid of it, Jim. It's so queer."

"Do you know what I think you should do to put your mind at rest?"

"What?"

"Take Chris along to see old Dr. Webster tomorrow. Let him have a little talk with her."

"Do you think she's ill—in her mind?"

"Good heavens, no! But when we come across something that's a bit beyond us, it's as well to take professional advice."

Next day I took Chris to see Dr. Webster. I left her in the waiting room while I told him briefly about Harry. He nodded sympathetically, then said:

"It's a fairly unusual case, Mrs. James, but by no means unique. I've had several cases of children's imaginary companions becoming so real to them that the parents got the jitters. I expect she's rather a lonely little girl, isn't she?"

"She doesn't know any other children. We're new to the neighbourhood, you see. But that will be put right when she starts school."

"And I think you'll find that when she goes to school and meets other children, these fantasies will disappear. You see, every child needs company of her own age, and if she doesn't get it, she invents it. Older people who are lonely talk to themselves. That doesn't mean that they're crazy, just that they need to talk to someone. A child is more practical. Seems silly to talk to oneself, she thinks, so she invents someone to talk to. I honestly don't think you've anything to worry about."

"That's what my husband says."

"I'm sure he does. Still, I'll have a chat with Christine as you've brought her. Leave us alone together."

I went to the waiting-room to fetch Chris. She was at the window. She said: "Harry's waiting."

"Where, Chris?" I said quietly, wanting suddenly to see with her eyes.

"There. By the rose bush."

The doctor had a bush of white roses in his garden.

"There's no one there," I said. Chris gave me a glance of unchildlike scorn. "Dr. Webster wants to see you now, darling," I said shakily. "You remember him, don't you? He gave you sweets when you were getting better from chicken pox."

"Yes," she said and went willingly enough to the doctor's surgery. I waited restlessly. Faintly I heard their voices through the wall, heard the doctor's chuckle, Christine's high peal of laughter. She was talking away to the doctor in a way she didn't talk to me.

When they came out, he said: "Nothing wrong with her whatever. She's just an imaginative little monkey. A word of advice, Mrs. James. Let her talk about Harry. Let her become accustomed to confiding in you. I gather you've shown some disapproval of this 'brother' of hers so she doesn't talk much to you about him. He makes wooden toys, doesn't he, Chris?"

"Yes, Harry makes wooden toys."

"And he can read and write, can't he?"

"And swim and climb trees and paint pictures. Harry can do everything. He's a wonderful brother." Her little face flushed with adoration.

The doctor patted me on the shoulder and said: "Harry sounds a very nice brother for her. He's even got red hair like you, Chris, hasn't he?"

"Harry's got red hair," said Chris proudly, "Redder than my hair. And he's nearly as tall as Daddy only thinner. He's as tall as you, Mummy. He's fourteen. He says he's tall for his age. What *is* tall for his age?"

"Mummy will tell you about that as you walk home," said Dr. Webster. "Now, goodbye, Mrs. James. Don't worry. Just let her prattle. Goodbye, Chris. Give my love to Harry."

"He's there," said Chris, pointing to the doctor's garden. "He's been waiting for me."

Dr Webster laughed. "They're incorrigible, aren't they?" he said. "I knew one poor mother whose children invented a whole tribe of imaginary natives whose rituals and taboos ruled the household. Perhaps you're lucky, Mrs. James!"

I tried to feel comforted by all this, but I wasn't. I hoped sincerely that when Chris started school this wretched Harry business would finish.

Chris ran ahead of me. She looked up as if at someone beside her. For a brief, dreadful second, I saw a shadow on the pavement alongside her own—a long, thin shadow—like a boy's shadow. Then it was gone. I ran to catch up and held her hand tightly all the way home. Even in the comparative security of the house—the house so strangely cold in this hot weather—I never let her out of my sight. On the face of it she behaved no differently toward me, but in reality she was drifting away. The child in my house was becoming a stranger.

For the first time since Jim and I had adopted Chris, I wondered seriously: Who is she? Where does she come from? Who were her real parents? Who is this little loved stranger I've taken as a daughter? Who *is* Christine?

Another week passed. It was Harry, Harry all the time. The day before she was to start school, Chris said:

"Not going to school."

"You're going to school tomorrow, Chris. You're looking forward to it. You know you are. There'll be lots of other little girls and boys."

"Harry says he can't come too."

"You won't want Harry at school. He'll—" I tried hard to follow the doctor's advice and appear to believe in Harry—"He'll be too old. He'd feel silly among little boys and girls, a great lad of fourteen."

"I won't go to school without Harry. I want to be with Harry." She began to weep loudly, painfully.

"Chris, stop this nonsense! Stop it!" I struck her sharply on the arm. Her crying ceased immediately. She stared at me, her blue eyes wide open and frighteningly cold. She gave me an adult stare that made me tremble. Then she said:

"You don't love me. Harry loves me. Harry wants me. He says I can go with him."

"I will not hear any more of this!" I shouted, hating the anger in my voice, hating myself for being angry at all with a little girl—*my* little girl—mine—

I went down on one knee and held out my arms.

"Chris, darling, come here."

She came slowly. "I love you," I said. "I love you, Chris, and I'm real. School is real. Go to school to please me."

"Harry will go away if I do."

"You'll have other friends."

"I want Harry." Again the tears, wet against my shoulder now. I held her closely.

"You're tired, baby. Come to bed."

She slept with the tear stains still on her face.

It was still daylight. I went to the window to draw her curtains. Golden shadows and long strips of sunshine in the garden. Then, again like a dream, the long thin clear-cut shadow of a boy near the white roses. Like a mad woman I opened the window and shouted:

"Harry! Harry!"

I thought I saw a glimmer of red among the roses, like close red curls on a boy's head. Then there was nothing.

When I told Jim about Christine's emotional outburst he said: "Poor little kid. It's always a nervy business, starting school. She'll be all right once she gets there. You'll be hearing less about Harry too, as time goes on."

"Harry doesn't want her to go to school."

"Hey! You sound as if you believe in Harry yourself!"

"Sometimes I do."

"Believing in evil spirits in your old age?" he teased me. But his eyes were concerned. He thought I was going "round the bend," and small blame to him!

"I don't think Harry's evil," I said. "He's just a boy. A boy who doesn't exist, except for Christine. And who *is* Christine?"

"None of that!" said Jim sharply. "When we adopted Chris we decided she was to be our own child. No probing into the past. No wondering and worrying. No mysteries. Chris is as much ours as if she'd been born of our flesh. Who is Christine, indeed! She's our daughter—and just you remember that!"

"Yes, Jim, you're right. Of course you're right."

He'd been so fierce about it that I didn't tell him what I planned to do the next day while Chris was at school.

Next morning Chris was silent and sulky. Jim joked with her and tried to cheer her, but all she would do was look out of the window and say: "Harry's gone."

"You won't need Harry now. You're going to school," said Jim.

Chris gave him that look of grown-up contempt she'd given me sometimes.

She and I didn't speak as I took her to school. I was almost in tears. Although I was glad for her to start school, I felt a sense of loss at parting with her. I suppose every mother feels that when she takes her ewe-lamb to school for the first time. It's the end of babyhood for the child, the beginning of life in reality, life with its cruelty, its strangeness, its barbarity. I kissed her goodbye at the gate and said:

"You'll be having dinner at school with the other children, Chris, and I'll call for you when school is over, at three o'clock."

"Yes, Mummy." She held my hand tightly. Other nervous little children were arriving with equally nervous parents. A pleasant young teacher with fair hair and a white linen dress appeared at the gate. She gathered the new children towards her and led them away. She gave me a sympathetic smile as she passed and said: "We'll take good care of her."

I felt quite light-hearted as I walked away, knowing that Chris was safe and I didn't have to worry.

Now I started on my secret mission. I took a bus to town and went to the big, gaunt building I hadn't visited for over five years. Then, Jim and I had gone together. The top floor of the building belonged to the Greythorne Adoption Society. I climbed the four flights and knocked on the familiar door with its scratched paint. A secretary whose face I didn't know let me in.

"May I see Miss Cleaver? My name is Mrs. James."

"Have you an appointment?"

"No, but it's very important."

"I'll see." The girl went out and returned a second later. "Miss Cleaver will see you, Mrs. James."

Miss Cleaver, a tall, thin, gray-haired woman with a charming smile, a plain, kindly face and a very wrinkled brow, rose to meet me. "Mrs. James. How nice to see you again. How is Christine?"

"She's very well. Miss Cleaver, I'd better get straight to the point. I know you don't normally divulge the origin of a child to its adopters and vice versa, but I must know who Christine is."

"Sorry, Mrs. James," she began, "our rules…"

"Please let me tell you the whole story, then you'll see I'm not just suffering from vulgar curiosity."

I told her about Harry.

When I'd finished, she said: "It's very queer. Very queer indeed.

Mrs. James, I'm going to break my rule for once. I'm going to tell you in strict confidence where Christine came from.

"She was born in a very poor part of London. There were four in the family: father, mother, son, and Christine herself."

"Son?"

"Yes. He was fourteen when—when it happened."

"When what happened?"

"Let me start at the beginning. The parents hadn't really wanted Christine. The family lived in one room at the top of an old house which should have been condemned by the Sanitary Inspector, in my opinion. It was difficult enough when there were only three of them, but with the baby as well life became a nightmare. The mother was a neurotic creature, slatternly, unhappy, too fat. After she'd had the baby she took no interest in it. The brother, however, adored the little girl from the start. He got into trouble for cutting school so he could look after her.

"The father had a steady job in a warehouse, not much money, but enough to keep them alive. Then he was sick for several weeks and lost his job. He was laid up in that messy room, ill, worrying, nagged by his wife, irked by the baby's crying and his son's eternal fussing over the child—I got all these details from neighbours afterwards, by the way. I was also told that he'd had a particularly bad time in the war and had been in a nerve hospital for several months before he was fit to come home at all after his demob. Suddenly it all proved too much for him.

"One morning, in the small hours, a woman in the ground floor saw something fall past her window and heard a thud on the ground. She went out to look. The son of the family was there on the ground. Christine was in his arms. The boy's neck was broken. He was dead. Christine was blue in the face but still breathing faintly.

"The woman woke the household, sent for the police and the doctor, then they went to the top room. They had to break down the door, which was locked and sealed inside. An overpowering smell of gas greeted them, in spite of the open window.

"They found husband and wife dead in bed and a note from the husband saying:

> I can't go on. I am going to kill them all.
> It's the only way.

"The police concluded that he'd sealed up door and windows and turned on the gas when his family was asleep, then lain beside his wife until he drifted into unconsciousness and death. But the son must have wakened. Perhaps he struggled with the door but couldn't open it. He'd be too weak to shout. All he could do was pluck away from the window, open it, fling himself out, holding his adored little sister tightly in his arms.

"Why Christine herself wasn't gassed is rather a mystery. Perhaps her head was right under the bedclothes, pressed against her brother's chest—they always slept together. Anyway, the child was taken to hospital, then to the home where you and Mr. James first saw her…and a lucky day that was for little Christine!"

"So her brother saved her life and died himself?" I said.

"Yes. He was a very brave young man."

"Perhaps he thought not so much of saving her as of keeping her with him. Oh dear! That sounds ungenerous. I didn't mean to be. Miss Cleaver, what was his name?"

"I'll have to look that up for you." She referred to one of her many files and said at last: "The family's name was Jones and the fourteen-year-old brother was called 'Harold.'"

"And did he have red hair?" I murmured.

"That I don't know, Mrs. James."

"But it's Harry. The boy was Harry. What does it mean? I can't understand it."

"It's not easy, but I think perhaps deep in her unconscious mind Christine has always remembered Harry, the companion of her babyhood. We don't think of children as having much memory, but there must be images of the past tucked away somewhere in their little heads. Christine doesn't *invent* this Harry. She *remembers* him. So clearly that she's almost brought him to life again. I know it sounds far-fetched, but the whole story is so odd that I can't think of any other explanation."

"May I have the address of the house where they lived?"

She was reluctant to give me this information, but I persuaded her and set out at last to find No. 13 Canver Row, where the man Jones had tried to kill himself and his whole family and almost succeeded.

The house seemed deserted. It was filthy and derelict. But one thing made me stare and stare. There was a tiny garden. A scatter of bright uneven grass splashed the bald brown patches of earth. But the little garden had one strange glory that none of the other houses in the poor sad street possessed—a bush of white roses. They bloomed gloriously. Their scent was overpowering.

I stood by the bush and stared up at the top window.

A voice startled me: "What are you doing here?"

It was an old woman, peering from the ground floor window.

"I thought the house was empty," I said.

"Should be. Been condemned. But they can't get me out. Nowhere else to go. Won't go. The others went quickly enough after it happened. No one else wants to come. They say the place is haunted. So it is. But what's the fuss about? Life and death.

They're very close. You get to know that when you're old. Alive or dead. What's the difference?"

She looked at me with yellowish, bloodshot eyes and said: "I saw him fall past my window. That's where he fell. Among the roses. He still comes back. I see him. He won't go away until he gets her."

"Who—who are you talking about?"

"Harry Jones. Nice boy he was. Red hair. Very thin. Too determined though. Always got his own way. Loved Christine too much, I thought. Died among the roses. Used to sit down here with her for hours, by the roses. Then died there. Or do people die? The church ought to answer, but it doesn't. Not one you can believe. Go away, will you? This place isn't for you. It's for the dead who aren't dead, and the living who aren't alive. Am I alive or dead? You tell me. I don't know."

The crazy eyes staring at me beneath the matted white fringe of hair frightened me. Mad people are terrifying. One can pity them, but one is still afraid. I murmured:

"I'll go now. Goodbye," and tried to hurry across the hard hot pavement, although my legs felt heavy and half-paralysed, as in a nightmare.

The sun blazed down on my head, but I was hardly away of it. I lost all sense of time or place as I stumbled on.

Then I heard something that chilled my blood.

A clock struck three.

At three o'clock I was supposed to be at the school gates, waiting for Christine.

Where was I now? How near the school? What bus should I take?

I made frantic inquiries of passers-by, who looked at me fearfully, as I had looked at the old woman. They must have thought I was crazy.

At last I caught the right bus, and sick with dust, petrol fumes and fear, reached the school. I ran across the hot, empty playground. In a classroom, the young teacher in white was gathering her books together.

"I've come for Christine James. I'm her mother. I'm so sorry I'm late. Where is she?" I gasped.

"Christine James?" the girl frowned, then said brightly: "Oh, yes, I remember, the pretty little red-haired girl. That's all right, Mrs. James. Her brother called for her. How alike they are, aren't they? And so devoted. It's rather sweet to see a boy of that age so fond of his baby sister. Has your husband got red hair, like the two children?"

"What did—her brother—say?" I asked faintly.

"He didn't say anything. When I spoke to him, he just smiled. They'll be home by now, I should think. I say, do you feel all right?"

"Yes, thank you. I must go home."

I ran all the way home through the burning streets.

"Chris! Christine, where are you? Chris! Chris!" Sometimes even now I hear my own voice of the past screaming through the cold house. "Christine! Chris! Where are you? Answer me! Chrrriiiiiss!" Then: "Harry! Don't take her away! Come back! Harry! Harry!"

Demented, I rushed out into the garden. The sun struck me like a hot blade. The roses glared whitely. The air was so still I seemed to stand in timelessness, placelessness. For a moment, I seemed very near to Christine, although I couldn't see her. Then the roses danced before my eyes and turned red. The world turned red. Blood red. Wet red. I fell through redness to blackness to nothingness—to almost death.

For weeks I was in bed with sunstroke, which turned to brain fever. During that time Jim and the police searched for Christine in vain. The futile search continued for months. The papers were full of the strange disappearance of the red-haired child. The teacher described the "brother" who had called for her. There were newspaper stories of kidnapping, baby snatching, child murders.

Then the sensation died down. Just another unsolved mystery in police files.

And only two people knew what had happened. An old crazed woman living in a derelict house, and myself.

Years have passed. But I walk in fear.

Such ordinary things make me afraid. Sunshine. Sharp shadows on grass. White roses. Children with red hair. And the name—Harry. Such an ordinary name.

We Three Ghosts of Halloween

(sung to the tune of "We Three Kings")

We three ghosts of Halloween are
Scaring kids who wander too far.
Trick or treating, candy eating,
Watching for the Halloween Star.
Oh...oh...
Star of darkness, star of fright,
Star of every gruesome sight,
West winds howling, cats a-yowling,
Let us play some tricks tonight.

boo!

o o o o

a a a a

II

Cold As Clay

Jennifer Brown was the daughter of the wealthiest farmer in the county. Mr. Brown loved his daughter more than anything on this earth and would have done anything for her. When Jennifer was eighteen, she fell in love with one of her father's farmhands, a local boy from a poor family, named Jim. Their romance blossomed, and soon they talked of marriage. But when Mr. Brown found out about the affair, he was furious. He did not think that Jim was nearly good enough for his daughter. "You will not marry that boy!" he scolded her.

"But I love him, Father," she protested.

"My decision is final," he said. And to keep them apart, he sent Jennifer away to live with her uncle on the other side of the county. Jim was a good hand on the farm, and Mr. Brown did not want to dismiss him. And he knew that even if he fired Jim, he would still be close enough to see her. To send her away was the best solution.

Jim stayed on, but was heartbroken, and his work soon began to suffer. He moped around and could not bring himself to care about anything but his lost love. He was sick with despair. Mr. Brown warned Jim if he did not change his ways, he would have to let him go. "I'll need your help at harvest time," Brown told him. But Jim only got worse. By October, Mr. Brown informed Jim that he had found another farmhand to take his place, that he was no longer wanted on the farm.

"But, Mr. Brown, please," said Jim, "I need this job. I can get better."

"I've given you enough chances," said Mr. Brown. "My decision is final."

Jim walked home that night, knowing that he would probably never see the Browns' farm or Jennifer again. It was an unusually cold, dark night with no moon in the sky, and Jim felt as low and miserable as a man can. In the dark, he did not see the pit on the side of the road. He tripped over an exposed root and fell into the ditch, hitting his head on a heavy rock and knocking himself unconscious. He wasn't found till morning. But by then, he had died of exposure.

Many in the town said that he'd died of a broken heart, and Mr. Brown felt so ashamed about the boy's death that he didn't tell Jennifer one word about it. In her uncle's house, she continued to pine for Jim and fantasize about the life they would have together someday.

One night about a month later, there came a loud knocking on her uncle's door. When Jennifer opened the door, Jim was standing outside, looking pale and disheveled.

"Your father asked me to come get you," he said. "He lent me his best horse."

"What is it, Jim, what's going on?"

"You need to come back with me," is all Jim would say.

She put on a coat and climbed onto the horse behind Jim, clinging tightly to his waist as they rode. Though the horse was galloping madly, Jim's body was still. After riding half the way back to the Browns' farm, Jim started to complain of a headache. "It aches something awful," he said.

She put her hand to his forehead and shuddered. "Why, you're as cold as clay," she said. "Are you ill?"

"It is just a headache," he said.

Jennifer took a red handkerchief from out of her coat pocket and wrapped it around Jim's head, hoping it would warm him.

They traveled so fast that they made it back to her father's farm in only a few hours. When they got to the front of the house, Jennifer climbed down from the horse, ran to the door, and knocked. When her father answered, he was shocked to see her.

"Didn't you send for me?" she asked.

"No, my dear, I did not," he said.

"But Jim told me you had, and he brought me all the way here from Uncle's," she said.

"Jim...brought you?" her father said, confused and a little frightened.

When Jennifer turned to show her father Jim and the horse, they were gone. She and her father checked the stable, and the horse was there, wet and trembling. But Jim was nowhere to be found. Mr. Brown confessed to his daughter what had happened, how he had fired Jim and how he had died on the side of the road. "Jim is alive," she said. "Don't you think I know him? Who brought me here if not Jim?" Mr. Brown did not know what to say.

Jennifer and her father traveled to the house of Jim's parents. His mother and father were amazed at her story and reluctantly agreed to open his grave. After they finally unearthed his coffin, they drew back the lid of his casket. Jennifer recoiled in horror as she laid eyes on Jim's decomposing corpse. And she screamed when she saw that he was wearing the red handkerchief she had wrapped around his head a few hours before.

Make Your Front Yard a Graveyard

1. Cut out various sizes and shapes of headstones from cardboard, plywood, or thick (4–5 inches) styrofoam, which you can get from a hardware/home improvement store. (See examples of shapes below.) For cutting plywood, a handsaw or jigsaw will be needed; for the styrofoam, you'll need a very sharp knife or jigsaw (cutting the tombstones is obviously not a project for the kids).
2. Apply a coat of gray primer and wait for it to dry. Paint the tombstones using sponges with gray, white, and black paint, or a gray or marble-textured spray paint. Then neatly write on them with black marker or paint an appropriate epitaph. Some good epitaphs include:

    Ben Dismembered—RIP (Rest in Pieces)
    I Told You I Was Sick
    Barry DaLive
    Yul B. Next
    Here Lies the Body of Lester Moore. No Les. No Moore.

3. Stake them into the grass in your front yard using metal or plastic rods. (For an added bit of ghoulishness, you could even stand up old pairs of gloves in front of the headstones to make it look like the hands of the deceased trying to crawl out from their graves.)

The Raven

nevermore

12

by Edgar Allan Poe

nevermore

nevermore

nevermore

nevermore

nevermore

nevermore

nevermore

nevermore

nevermore

nevermore

nevermore

nevermore

nevermore

nevermore

nevermore

nevermore

Once upon a midnight dreary, while I pondered, weak and weary,
Over many a quaint and curious volume of forgotten lore—
While I nodded, nearly napping, suddenly there came a tapping,
As of some one gently rapping, rapping at my chamber door.
"'Tis some visitor," I muttered, "tapping at my chamber door—
Only this and nothing more."

Ah, distinctly I remember it was in the bleak December,
And each separate dying ember wrought its ghost upon the floor.
Eagerly I wished the morrow;—vainly I had sought to borrow
From my books surcease of sorrow—sorrow for the lost Lenore—
For the rare and radiant maiden whom the angels name Lenore—
Nameless here for evermore.

And the silken sad uncertain rustling of each purple curtain
Thrilled me—filled me with fantastic terrors never felt before;
So that now, to still the beating of my heart, I stood repeating:
"'Tis some visitor entreating entrance at my chamber door—

Some late visitor entreating entrance at my chamber door;
This it is and nothing more."

Presently my soul grew stronger; hesitating then no longer,
"Sir," said I, "or Madam, truly your forgiveness I implore;
But the fact is I was napping, and so gently you came rapping,
And so faintly you came tapping, tapping at my chamber door,
That I scarce was sure I heard you"—here I opened wide the door—
Darkness there and nothing more.

Deep into that darkness peering, long I stood there wondering, fearing,
Doubting, dreaming dreams no mortals ever dared to dream before;
But the silence was unbroken, and the stillness gave no token,
And the only word there spoken was the whispered word, "Lenore?"
This I whispered, and an echo murmured back the word, "Lenore!"—
Merely this and nothing more.

Back into the chamber turning, all my soul within me burning,
Soon again I heard a tapping something louder than before.
"Surely," said I, "surely that is something at my window lattice;
Let me see, then, what thereat is, and this mystery explore—
Let my heart be still a moment, and this mystery explore;—
'Tis the wind and nothing more.

Open here I flung the shutter, when, with many a flirt and flutter,

In there stepped a stately Raven of the saintly days of yore.
Not the least obeisance made he; not a minute stopped or stayed he,
But, with mien of lord or lady, perched above my chamber door—
Perched upon a bust of Pallas just above my chamber door—
Perched, and sat, and nothing more.

Then the ebony bird beguiling my sad fancy into smiling,
By the grave and stern decorum of the countenance it wore,
"Though thy crest be shorn and shaven, thou," I said, "art sure no craven,
Ghastly grim and ancient Raven wandering from the Nightly shore—
Tell me what thy lordly name is on the Night's Plutonian shore!"
Quoth the Raven, "Nevermore."

Much I marvelled this ungainly fowl to hear discourse so plainly,
Though its answer little meaning—little relevancy bore;
For we cannot help agreeing that no living human being
Ever yet was blessed with seeing bird above his chamber door—
Bird or beast upon the sculptured bust above his chamber door,
With such name as "Nevermore."

But the Raven, sitting lonely on that placid bust, spoke only
That one word, as if its soul in that one word he did outpour.
Nothing farther then he uttered; not a feather then he fluttered—
Till I scarcely more than muttered: "Other friends have flown before—
On the morrow *he* will leave me, as my Hopes have flown before."
Then the bird said, "Nevermore."

Startled at the stillness broken by reply so aptly spoken,
"Doubtless," said I, "what it utters is its only stock and store,
Caught from some unhappy master whom unmerciful Disaster
Followed fast and followed faster till his songs one burden bore—
Till the dirges of his Hope that melancholy burden bore
Of 'Never—nevermore.'"

But the Raven still beguiling all my sad soul into smiling,
Straight I wheeled a cushioned seat in front of bird and bust and door;
Then, upon the velvet sinking, I betook myself to linking
Fancy unto fancy, thinking what this ominous bird of yore—
What this grim, ungainly, ghastly, gaunt, and ominous bird of yore
Meant in croaking "Nevermore."

This I sat engaged in guessing, but no syllable expressing
To the fowl whose fiery eyes now burned into my bosom's core;
This and more I sat divining, with my head at ease reclining
On the cushion's velvet lining that the lamp-light gloated o'er,
But whose velvet violet lining with the lamp-light gloating o'er
She shall press, ah, nevermore!

Then, methought, the air grew denser, perfumed from an unseen censer
Swung by Seraphim whose foot-falls tinkled on the tufted floor.
"Wretch," I cried, "thy God hath lent thee—by these angels he hath sent thee
Respite—respite and nepenthe from thy memories of Lenore!
Quaff, oh quaff this kind nepenthe and forget this lost Lenore!"
Quoth the Raven, "Nevermore."

"Prophet!" said I, "thing of evil!—prophet still, if bird or devil!—
Whether Tempter sent, or whether tempest tossed thee here ashore,
Desolate, yet all undaunted, on this desert land enchanted—
On this home by Horror haunted,—tell me truly, I implore—
Is there—*is* there balm in Gilead?—tell me—tell me, I implore!"
Quoth the Raven, "Nevermore."

"Prophet!" said I, "thing of evil!—prophet still, if bird or devil!
By that Heaven that bends above us—by that God we both adore—
Tell this soul with sorrow laden if, within the distant Aidenn,
It shall clasp a sainted maiden whom the angels name Lenore—
Clasp a rare and radiant maiden whom the angels name Lenore."
Quoth the Raven, "Nevermore."

"Be that our sign of parting, bird or fiend!" I shrieked, upstarting—
"Get thee back into the tempest and the Night's Plutonian shore!
Leave no black plume as a token of that lie thy soul hath spoken!
Leave my loneliness unbroken!—quit the bust above my door!
Take thy beak from out my heart, and take thy form from off my door!"
Quoth the Raven, "Nevermore."

And the Raven, never flitting, still is sitting, still is sitting
On the pallid bust of Pallas just above my chamber door;
And his eyes have all the seeming of a demon's that is dreaming,
And the lamp-light o'er him streaming throws his shadows on the floor;
And my soul from out that shadow that lies floating on the floor
Shall be lifted—nevermore!

The End…

or Is It?

Bats in the Window

Using a drawing of the silhouette of a bat (like the ones below), make photocopies of the bat at various sizes, from small to very large. Then cut out 20–30 of the bat shapes. Stick them to your windows using Scotch tape with small bats at the bottom, fanning up and out gradually with larger ones, taping the largest ones at the top to make it look like bats are coming out of your house.

credits

Cover and text illustrations by Megan Dempster, Jenna Jakubowski, and Chris Pierik

All stories read by Pat Duke.

Audio recording, editing, engineering, and mastering by John Larson, Larson Recording, Chicago, Illinois.